MW01611305

Hesper Stalides and Felix Morlan have been best friends for as long as they can remember, bonding over their troubled home lives. When a horrible sports injury derails Felix's promising career and results in the loss of his scholarship, Hesper offers a proposition: a year-long marriage of convenience so he can get free tuition at the college where she works.

It isn't supposed to be complicated...until they fall in love for real. When Hesper reveals that she's asexual, Felix must reassess everything he thinks about love and ask himself what he's willing to sacrifice for a future with Hesper—before the past she's spent her life running from can take her away from him forever.

ACE OF

HEARTS

LUCY MASON

A NineStar Press Publication

www.ninestarpress.com

Ace of Hearts

First Edition, October 2022

ISBN: 978-1-64890-553-7

Also available in eBook, ISBN: 978-1-64890-552-0

CONTENT WARNING:
This book contains depictions of abuse of an adult child by a parent, stalking/harassment, kidnapping/abduction, references to alcohol abuse, and vomiting.

*To everyone who's ever thought they're broken.
You're not. You deserve to take up space and be loved
exactly as you are.*

Wednesday, 6:42 PM

Yay sports! Do the thing! Win the points!

10:39 PM

37-24. Going to regionals!

Thursday, 10:13 AM

Did you hear about the pickle incident in the cafeteria?

10:13 AM

???

10:15 AM

It was kind of a big DILL

10:15 AM

Get it?

10:16 AM

DILL? Ba-dum-CHA!

10:17 AM

OH MY GOD, FELIX, we can't be friends anymore.

10:23 AM

Don't be jealous just because my pun game is so strong ;D

11:11 AM

Make a wish.

11:12 AM

I always do.

Yesterday, 7:16 PM

GO GO REGIONALS GO!

11:10 PM

SO? How did the game go?

11:41 PM

Felix?

11:53 PM

Everything okay?

Today, 12:18 AM

You've NEVER not answered. Please let me know you're safe.

12:39 AM

I'm going to start calling the hospitals and morgues and I'll kill you if you were just at home sleeping off the game and ignoring me!

12:42 AM

Felix. I'm scared.

12:42 AM

Please be okay.

CHAPTER ONE

HESPER

IT WAS NOT my Felix Morlan lying in the hospital bed, tangled in the sterile white sheets. He was the bravest, funniest, most cheerful man I knew, strong enough to make up for it when his friends were weak, and this wasn't him. I brushed his dark hair away from his forehead, which was glistening with sweat, pain hazing over his eyes.

"Sorry I scared you, Hes." His voice cracked, and I handed him a Styrofoam cup filled with cold water and ice chips.

"I'm just glad you're…"

Okay? Of course he wasn't okay. One of his teammates had shown me a replay of the hit that had hyperextended his knee and destroyed his ACL. It had been on mute, and Felix was wearing a helmet that obscured part of his face, but the contorted expression of agony was seared into my memory. He may or may not have blacked out from the pain; I wasn't sure because I quit watching, unable to stomach it.

"Want me to call the nurse?" I asked tentatively.

He turned his head away, but not before I caught the shine of tears gathering in his eyes. His leg was wrapped heavily in dressings, but I'd seen it when he came out of surgery, exhausted but too frightened to sleep while I waited. The skin around his knee was swollen, an angry red color where staples held the surgical wounds closed. I'd sat by his bed, sketching on the small pad I kept in Calamity, my old Jeep, while he slept off the anesthesia. But he was awake now, and he twisted his calloused hands in the sheets.

"They'll be keeping me for observation for a few days. Go home and get some rest."

"Nope."

"Some of the guys from the team will stop by and—"

"*Nope*," I reiterated firmly, crossing my arms.

It was a policy we'd had with each other our whole lives, and it didn't change even when we'd moved halfway across the country together for college: we had nobody else here, but we had each other. He'd watched my back, and I would watch his. Felix and I had been best friends since we were old enough to walk and talk. Now, his mom was in jail while his dad was busy raising his six younger siblings, and I had run away from Missouri to avoid getting an order of protection against my own father. We'd basically raised each other. I wasn't running away at the first sign of trouble.

"Show me." He held out one hand for my sketch pad and

I clutched it to my chest. "Come on."

Normally this was fine. I'd draw tables covered in leaves, teacups and books and pocket watches and chunks of amethyst and rusty old keys, the kind of things I found aesthetically soothing. But I'd been doing something different while he slept, trying to erase the memory of his pain in the video replay of his injury. I'd drawn the slightly blocky angle of his jaw, his mouth turned up in half a smile, a five-o'clock shadow dusting the sides of his face. I'd drawn him *happy*, my best copy of the way he looked in my favorite memory of him.

I contemplated crumpling the page before he could see it.

Instead, I flipped back to an earlier page where I'd been doing a study of the trees outside his hospital window, light filtering through them in an orange haze as the sun rose. I hadn't been able to quite capture it with the small bag of pencils I had on hand, but it was enough that he got the idea.

"Remind me again why you aren't going into this?" He sounded clearer than he had in several hours, his eyes focused on my sketch pad. It was an uncomfortable feeling, to see someone marvel at my work. Like being under a microscope.

"No steady paycheck," I reminded him, counting the reasons I'd rehearsed to people a hundred thousand times off on my fingers. "Deadlines would push me to create when I didn't feel like it. I would grow to hate it if I had to do it for a living. The pressure would be too intense."

I didn't list the other reason. Sometimes it took every ounce of energy I possessed just to get up in the morning. Sometimes I simply didn't have enough inside me to both function *and* create. Art was my escape. If I turned it into another source of stress, where would I hide when the rest of the world got to be too much? What would I do to restore the balance?

"Those are all good reasons," he agreed begrudgingly, and he reached back over to hand the pad back to me, twisting slightly to do so.

He didn't say a word but the set of his mouth and eyebrows told me he'd moved wrong, in a way that would have left him screaming if he hadn't been so heavily medicated. My chest hurt, my lungs burning because I just couldn't get enough oxygen in, because I couldn't breathe looking at the way my best friend suffered. This was the sort of thing you read about in the paper or heard about on the news. It happened to other people, sure. But it wasn't supposed to happen to Felix.

1Despite the chill outside, Calamity's seats were sticky with heat from the afternoon sun when I left the hospital, and I wiggled my phone charger in the adapter, praying it would connect. I ran the battery down the night before, frantically making calls to find out what had happened and where Felix was, and I'd sent one semi-panicked email to my boss explaining I wouldn't be in today, but I wasn't prepared for the onslaught of messages when the screen lit back up. I scrolled through them, my stomach clenching as I read increasingly worried and annoyed messages. I closed out of the message app and pulled up the internet browser. It was like worrying at a sore tooth: even though I knew it would be awful, I had to look. I had to know what Felix was going back to.

The answer, it seemed, was not much.

There was already an online article plastered on the local news channel's website: *Mustangs Star Athlete Suffers Career-Ending Injury During Championship Game*. I cringed but kept reading. There were pictures. There was speculation on whether the opposing team had intentionally caused the injury. It had happened in the third quarter, and rather than stopping the game, they put in a backup player and went on to narrowly win. It even ended on a celebratory note, advertising the time and date of the next playoff game, like Felix's whole world hadn't just changed. I scrolled back up to the top of the page.

Career-ending.

Career-ending.

Oh, God.

My phone started to ring, and I shoved it under the jacket in the passenger seat, counting my breaths and turning the key as the Jeep roared to life, sputtering a little sadly. Emails were fine, text messages were even better, but phone calls hit me funny sometimes, and after the nightmare of the last twenty-four hours I couldn't bear the thought of talking—or trying to hear—on a cell phone. I rolled the windows down and turned up the music and let the wind dry the tears from my face. Art was my refuge, but solo driving time was my freedom.

Zzzzt.

Zzzzzt, zzzzzt.

I slammed the radio's off button. Gravel popped as I turned Calamity's wheel sharply, pulling off onto the shoulder because whoever was calling wouldn't stop. Felix's phone was still in the locker room. What if it was his dad calling? What if someone back home had heard? What if it was a nurse calling saying *something has gone horribly wrong, come back immediately*? What if he needed me? What if, what if, what if?

As soon as I accepted the call, I regretted it. My boss was the father figure I never had, and he worried about me like I was his own daughter. Which was great, until it wasn't.

"Hesper Elise Stalides, you could have been dead in a ditch and I wouldn't have known!"

I flinched. "Sorry, Zach."

His voice softened marginally—he knew about my phone anxiety. He spoke slowly and clearly, not in a condescending way, but enough that I didn't have to ask him to repeat himself. "I got your message that you were on your way to see your friend and you wouldn't be in today. How is he?"

I squeezed my eyes shut, and the hand that wasn't holding the phone to my ear spasmed against the steering wheel, turning my knuckles ashy white.

"Oh, he'll recover. Eventually. But I don't think he'll ever play football again."

Saying it out loud made it seem real. I couldn't imagine Felix without sports. He had initially pursued it because he knew it was the only way he could ever afford college—I felt so betrayed when he chose athletic extracurriculars over art and band with me—but it had turned into a genuine fire and passion for him. It was his *thing*.

And now it was gone.

"I'm sorry to hear that. Are you on your way home?"

"Yeah."

"Do me a favor and let me know when you get there safe."

"I will. Thanks for understanding."

Zach hung up without saying goodbye, because goodbye was simply not a thing he did. He had told me once his grandpa would say "uh-huh" before hanging up but said any kind of farewell had too much finality. This old superstition had carried over the generations of their family. It was just a fact that my boss hung up on me every single time he called.

"There," I said out loud to the empty, silent car. "I answered the phone and it wasn't that bad. Stop being such a drama queen about it."

But it didn't feel like I was being dramatic. Talking on the phone made it feel like all the air had left my lungs, and I was suffocating, and my brain couldn't process the words the person on the other end was saying, and then I had to ask them to repeat themselves, and they said it again, but I still couldn't understand and they were starting to get annoyed and—

Stop. Now is not the time for an anxiety spiral. Pull it together.

Windows down. Music up. I picked up my phone and texted Zach.

4:39 PM

I'll get back in 40 mins. Meet at Cass's for dinner?

I didn't receive an answer, because he wasn't a texting sort of man. He regularly sent me messages that said *brb*—

as if I'd notice he was leaving his phone for a minute when we were miles apart. All the same, when I got back to town he was there at our usual table, his glasses low on his nose and thick eyebrows creased downward, tapping a pen (the audacity! A permanent ink pen!) on the sudoku puzzle in the newspaper on the table. I dropped my messenger bag and collapsed in the seat across from him. I was too tired, as if I'd run a marathon instead of sitting at my best friend's bedside all night.

"You look rough."

"Thanks, Zach, that's sweet."

He glared at me over his glasses. "Next time let me know you made it safe, okay?"

"Hopefully there won't *be* a next time."

"So, what's your friend gonna do?"

I put my face in my hands. "Beats me. He's gonna be so lost without football, and that scholarship was all he had. I mean, he has a work-study job with the college's mainte-nance department, but…" I slid my phone across the table, the article pulled up on the browser.

Zach cringed with every new detail he read.

"Maybe they'll let him finish out his degree," he said doubtfully. My phone buzzed in his hands. "'Hey, H. Jack-son brought my phone. Text when you can.' Is this the guy?"

I snatched my phone back. Adults didn't understand what an invasion of privacy it was when they read your text messages. Despite the fact that I was twenty-one, almost twenty-two, I still thought of everyone else as a grown-up and myself as just…not. *I'm an adult! I* am *a grown-up! I pay bills and have a job!* But it was like there was some se-cret rite of passage to figuring out life as a grown-up, and nobody had let me in on it, so I was stuck in limbo forever.

"You've heard me talk about him before. We grew up together, moved out here together."

"H?" His sizable eyebrows disappeared under his bangs.

"Yes! H, Hes, Hesper. I answer to any. This is not a surprise; you've known me for three years."

"And he spells out all the words like you do."

"Yes, like a civilized human who doesn't think it's too much extra effort to put the Y and the O before the U to spell you." I stared pointedly at him, but as usual, my criticism didn't faze him. I hated text speak.

The server, a cute blonde girl with a mean streak for most people but a soft spot for her regular customers, brought me a glass of sweet tea, ice cubes clinking merrily.

"With *sugar*." Zach shuddered. "Appalling."

While technically I was from the Midwest, we were *very* southern in how we took our tea. I liked it as sweet as hummingbird water; my "bless your heart" was almost always a passive-aggressive dig; I knew how to square-dance (badly), thanks to high school PE classes. You can take the girl out of Missouri, but you can't take Missouri out of the girl.

Zach caught me up on all the library drama of the day while I made appropriate noises of rage (a student was caught eating with greasy potato chip fingers while they were handling an expensive book) and disgust (another student brought back DVDs covered in a questionable, sticky, yellow substance of unknown origin.) He had a strict no-phones-during-dinner policy, but I surreptitiously tapped out messages to Felix on my lap. If he saw me, he decided to let it slide given the circumstances, because he cheerfully chattered while we ate.

6:02 PM

I'm home. Ish.

> **6:02 PM**
>
> *I'm in the hospital. Ish.*
>
> **6:04 PM**
>
> *Zach freaked, y/y?*

Zach only knew about Felix in passing, but Felix knew all about Zach, because I told him everything—well, most things—for almost forever. I mean, the boy taught me to tie my shoes; I spent summers showing his little sisters how to swim; he didn't abandon me even when we went to prom and I spent most of the night in the bathroom, shaking with my skirt bundled up in my arms and sucking in oxygen like it was running out. When he missed being crowned king because he was comforting me, he wasn't even mad, though I was mad enough at myself for both of us.

6:07 PM

You could say that. Need anything?

> **6:08 PM**
>
> *A burger. A milkshake. Anything but Jell-O and tasteless*

hospital cafeteria mashed potatoes.

6:08 PM

Seriously though. Get some rest.

He was worried about me—while he was laid up in a hospital bed with a shattered career and a decimated tendon and a boatload of pain. I had won the best-friend lottery. I didn't deserve him. Zach and I played rock-paper-scissors, our tradition for deciding who would pay, and though I could usually see his tells, he beat me fair and square. The server zipped his card through the register's reader, then handed it back to him along with an adding machine tape of the charges.

"You okay to drive home?"

"Yes, Zach."

"You won't fall asleep?"

"No, Zach."

"You stayed up all night with your friend."

I pinched the bridge of my nose, exhaling. My neck hurt and I was exhausted and everything was falling apart at the seams, but I smiled my most convincing smile. "I promise I'll be okay. And I'll let you know when I'm home."

"You better. See you at work Monday?"

"Nine sharp."

He saluted and lumbered off. He folded his six-foot-something frame into the tiny, banana-yellow car he had parallel parked by the side of the cafe. No matter how many times I watched him do it, the hilarity never wore off. I walked farther down the street to the parking lot, because I had passed my driving test but parking on the street seemed like more risk than I could afford to take. Calamity turned over once, twice, and finally roared to life. I patted the dashboard fondly. She was like me in a lot of ways: a quirky mess, a work in progress, broken but still worth keeping around.

The drive across campus was short. My house was tall but had the smallest footprint on the block—an old but cozy home with faded blue siding and a tiny porch with gingerbread detailing I repainted white every summer. A little flag saluted me—there were bills in the mailbox, because there were *always* bills. That was one part of adulthood that hadn't skipped out on me.

Phone bill. Light bill. Water bill. Political pamphlet. Coupons for a clothing store I seldom frequented because I hated shopping, but they had a nice pair of pants once. At the bottom of the pile, a hand-addressed envelope with handwriting I had hoped to never see again. The response was instinctive and instantaneous—my stomach lurched, and I hurled the envelope as hard as I could away from me, like somehow by being farther away it could hurt me less. It fluttered ineffectually to the floor.

It was so difficult to read I was surprised the post office had been able to deliver it. The pen had been pressed so hard into the paper it looked embossed. In the bottom right was the address, *my* address, that I had guarded so carefully. Seeing it written in that almost-illegible scrawl made me feel like climbing out of my own skin. I hated it. In the upper left was my father's address.

I was loath to touch it again, but I retrieved it from the old tan tile of the kitchen floor and sat at the table with it. I wanted to shred it, burn it, like destroying it would banish the overwhelming fear and dread that had seized me. *RETURN TO SENDER*. I put the words on it as big and bold as I could, then went back out into the dark October night and replaced it in the mailbox, raising the little flag so they would take it away the next morning. I trudged back inside, up the stairs, and threw myself down on my bed. The streetlights filtered in through the sheer navy curtains dotted with little silver stars. On my ceiling overhead, glowing stars and planets and comets shone faintly green in the darkness.

I was tired. I wanted to sleep. I *needed* to sleep. But I had reached that strung-out place of exhaustion where everything seemed a step removed, like I was watching the world through an external lens, and the sounds of my house were too loud and I longed for the soothing scent of my paints, which always reminded me strongly of tea leaves. Instead, I peeled off my hoodie and jeans stained with Alizarin Red and Phthalo Green oils and put on my most comfortable flannel pajamas, then rolled myself up in my blankets like a giant Hesper burrito.

But the weight of the thing in the mailbox pressed down on me, my breaths coming in jerky gasps too short for sleep. Somehow, despite my best attempts at invisibility, I had been found. This meant, of course, it was only a matter of time before he showed up on my doorstep to terrorize me in person.

1:34 AM

How much does a pirate pay

for corn?

Oh my God. There was no way he could know I was awake fending off a panic attack, but there he was, with his stupid jokes.

1:34 AM

Felix it is too late for puns

1:35 AM

Or too early

1:35 AM

Or something

1:35 AM

Shouldn't you be sleeping?

1:37 AM

A BUCK-AN-EAR!

1:42 AM

Yes, a spectacular feat of hilarity Felix, good NIGHT

1:51 AM

You know you love my puns.

1:54 AM

See you in the morning, H. Thank you.

I didn't love his puns, but dammit, I laughed in spite of myself, curling up and finally dropping off with the sound of it still in my ears.

CHAPTER TWO

FELIX

THE BEST THING about Hesper Stalides was that she knew how to coexist peacefully. When my team came to visit, they noisily crowded around, clamoring at top volume so that I couldn't understand any of them and an orderly stuck his head in, glaring, to shush them.

When Hes came, she always gave me exactly what I needed. Earlier in the morning she had squeezed onto the slim hospital bed beside me, careful to avoid my left leg, the tray over both our laps. We played cards—all my favorite games, BS and Speed and even War, which she usually hated. In the afternoon she retreated to a corner of the room, her sketchbook propped on her knees and at least three pencils stuck into the messy knot of curly hair on top of her head, her sneakers tapping out a rhythm to a song only she could hear. She didn't seem to notice I was watching, because when she started drawing the rest of the world ceased to exist for her. She said little, but that was fine. Her presence was familiar and comforting through the haze of pain and panic.

A nurse came in with a set of crutches, her face pinched with sympathy as she helped me wrestle my bandaged knee into a brace. I had grown up understanding everything came with a cost, most of which I couldn't afford, and everything in the room had a price tag. How much would the brace set me back? The crutches? The plastic bags of liquid they'd given me through an IV the day before? The sheer astronomical expense of it all made me queasy, especially since my bank account rarely exceeded a couple hundred bucks.

When I proved I could walk down the hall and back to my room on crutches, they began the process of discharging me. Hesper carried my small bag of belongings to her ratty old Jeep and held my crutches while I heaved myself up in the passenger seat. Even though it was cold out she cracked her window, wispy curls fluttering against her cheeks and forehead.

"You're being unusually quiet."

She was right—normally, I was the talkative one. She was always better at listening.

"Just thinking about how I'm gonna afford all this. I can only have my work-study job if I'm in classes, and I can only afford classes if I get to keep my scholarship." My stomach turned and I let my head thump against the headrest, gazing out at the blurry piles of red and gold leaves and the blue afternoon sky peeking through the almost bare tree branches. "And I only get to keep my scholarship if I can play the sport to go with it."

Her hands tightened on the wheel. "We'll figure something out. We'll get through this."

This was her mantra. When there was no way to get around something, even when it didn't feel like we'd make it, *we'll get through this*. Usually, it felt like the truth. This time, I wasn't sure which of us needed convincing: me or her. I had a card in my jacket pocket reminding me of my first physical therapy appointment, and it felt heavier than it should. It felt *expensive*.

She parked by the big, industrial gray building that served as dormitories, little white balconies jutting out on every floor with tiny chairs and tables crammed onto them.

The lobby was oppressively hot, overcompensating for the chill in the air outside, and we hustled into the elevator. It was so narrow my breath ruffled her hair, and she shifted my bag from hand to hand, watching the numbers over the door light up as we rose. I usually loved having a top-floor room—the view was amazing, nobody could stomp around on the floor above us all hours of the night, and running up and down the eight flights of stairs every day was a good workout. Now I felt trapped.

Jackson, my roommate and the best running back on our team, was waiting for me. He was surprisingly light on his feet for such a big guy—two hundred fifty pounds of solid muscle—and I'd heard he won the game for us. He grabbed me and pulled me into a bear hug.

"Congrats on the win." My voice came out strained; I

struggled to keep my balance on my crutches.

"Thanks, Felix."

He clapped my shoulder a few times before letting go of me and trying to go in for a hug with Hesper, but I hadn't warned him—she was funny about hugs. Or, actually, any sort of touching. She was mostly fine with me, but even that had taken years. She tactfully sidestepped and shook his hand, his enormous one dwarfing her small, crooked, paint-stained fingers, leaving him looking baffled.

"I think we met at the hospital," she said firmly, turning his hand loose and taking a step back.

"Oh! You're the girl he grew up with!" Jackson raised his eyebrows and looked over to me. "Damn, Felix, you didn't tell me she was this fine!"

The change in her demeanor was abrupt. She stepped back, eyes narrowed, cheeks reddening with anger or embarrassment or a healthy mix of both.

"*Damn*, Felix, you didn't tell me your roommate was so forward."

Jackson looked at me helplessly, but once Hesper got rolling there was no stopping her.

"I'm heading back home. It's a long drive."

"H—"

"Text me if you need anything." She acted like Jackson wasn't even in the room, whirling through the door and slamming it behind her.

"What did you do that for!"

"It was a *compliment*!" Jackson said defensively.

I hobbled over to the window and watched. It took her a long time to storm out of the double doors—she must have taken the stairs—and she slammed Calamity's door so hard the whole frame shook. She sat there for a long time, pulling herself together, before putting the Jeep in gear and driving away. I should have stopped her. I should have been right there in the seat beside her, instead of standing here with my dumbass roommate, who meant well but needed to learn how to read the room a little, for Christ's sake.

"You don't get to hit on my best friend!" If I thought I could do it without falling over, I would have whacked him with a crutch.

He held up his hands like he was warding off an attack. "You jealous, dude?"

"No, I'm mad! You upset her!"

"Sounds to me like you're jealous."

"I'm not having this discussion with you." I made my way over to the sofa, thought better of it, and went for a hard kitchen chair. Uncomfortable, but easier to get out of. "Have you talked to Coach Maze yet?"

He fidgeted, which was all the answer I needed. "Do you need anything? 'Cause I've got a study group—"

"Liar." Jackson was many things, including my friend, but he had never been part of a study group a day in his life. I rolled my eyes, and he slumped his shoulders.

"Yeah." He rubbed the back of his neck, refusing to meet my eyes. "Yeah, Coach came by last night."

"And what did he say?"

"Just for you to call him."

He didn't stick around, then I was alone in my dorm which would not be my dorm for very much longer, the only place I had known since leaving home. How many nights had I spent sitting on the floor with teammates piled around me, taking turns playing video games? Where would I go when they kicked me out?

Don't freak out. Everything is fixable.

So I did what I always did in times of trouble.

6:08 PM

*What's the difference be-
tween a hippo and a Zippo?*

6:10 PM

*A hippo is really heavy, and
a Zippo is a little lighter!*

6:18 PM

I'm sorry about Jackson.

I didn't get to see if she responded once she got home. (Every day she threatened to end our lifelong friendship over my love of puns, but I knew she secretly dug it—why else would she stick around for so many years?) There was a knock at the door and my coach slipped in, wearing the same guilty expression I'd seen on every fucking face since the game, but worse somehow, because he was about to take away my only shot at a future. I knew it, and he knew I knew it.

"Coach Maze," I greeted him, leaning hard against the table. I resisted the urge to ask if he was here to deliver the bad news.

"I'm sorry about your knee, Morlan." He hung his head. "How are you holdin' up?"

A flash of anger, there and gone—because how did he

think I was holding up? That ire was new. I had always been the easygoing friendly one, the oasis to Hesper's fiery temper.

"I'm...I'll make it." I shrugged.

"Don't worry about the surgery bill. The school's got insurance for that." He sat down at the table with me.

"They'd better." Deep, even breaths. This wasn't his fault. "Just tell me, Coach."

"You can finish out the semester on scholarship. I can put you on injured reserve next semester, but that's about all I can do. What did they say about when you'd be able to play again?"

Coward. He already knew. I scrubbed my hands against my face, too tired from the trauma and hungover from the pain medication to deal with this.

"At least a month of crutches. Months of intense physical rehab before I can walk without a brace. And it'll always be prone to reinjury. They repaired the ACL as best they could, but..." I swallowed. I hadn't said this next bit out loud to anyone, though I suspected they all knew it. "They advised against ever playing sports again, or next time the injury could be worse. If I hurt it again, I might lose the ability to walk."

He clenched his fists. "I hate to hear that, son."

I wanted to beg him, *just tell me, tell me it's over.* And more importantly, *tell me what to do next, because otherwise I'll have to move back home and I'll live my whole life and die in my backwater town.* My dad would be thrilled—we missed each other like crazy—but the only jobs there were gas station attendants and prison guards for the big local penitentiary. There was nothing wrong with those, but it wasn't *me*—and besides, how would *that* feel, to work at the jail where my mom had spent the last ten years?

"Are there any other scholarships? I have a 3.4 GPA." I was grasping at straws. "I'm a first-generation college student. I come from a single parent household. My mom is incarcerated. There's gotta be something."

He scrolled through his phone, scooting his chair up beside mine so we could both see. Every scholarship listing seemed to have a stipulation—and they all excluded me. *Graduated from a Pennsylvania high school* or *for freshmen only* or *with an interest in the field of engineering* or *students who have been a resident of Pennsylvania for at least five years.*

"Talk to financial aid tomorrow. See what they can do for you."

No reward for grades; no reward for being brave and moving across the United freaking States and knowing only one person but still making a life for myself. No reward for helping my dad raise my brother and sisters, or visiting my mom in jail on holidays and her birthday. The only thing I had of any value to the college was my athletic talent, and that was gone.

I was screwed.

TEN AGONIZING DAYS and countless hours in the financial aid office later, I finally got the answer. It wasn't a surprise, but it still hurt. I almost never called Hesper, because she hated talking on the phone, but this was kind of an emergency—she could forgive me this once. Jackson had been avoiding me and I was alone in the cramped little living room kitchen combo, my leg stretched out on the couch and only four days' worth of Percocet left in the little orange bottle in my medicine cabinet and an appointment reminder for Wednesday afternoon magnetted to the fridge door.

She picked up on the first ring, sounding vaguely panicked. She knew I didn't take calling her lightly.

"Felix! What's wrong?"

"I just need to talk. I need to talk this through," I rambled. "Because I'm about to be homeless and I don't want to go back to the middle of nowhere."

"Listen to me." Most of the time I held her together, but now that I was the one falling apart, I heard the steel in her voice. It was easy to forget she was strong for all the times she had almost, but not quite, broken. "You will not be homeless. Start packing."

I heard her keys jingling, Calamity's door opening and slamming shut again.

"Hesper—"

"I will be there in one hour. I can't talk and drive or I'd stay on the phone."

"I don't understand."

The engine sputtered, then turned over, but she spoke clearly over it. "You are my best friend and the only person I have ever trusted. You have seen me through hell and high water, and as long as I am alive you will always have a place to go, do you understand me?"

My chest hurt. "I—I don't know what to say."

"I think the words you're looking for are 'thank you.' I'm going to hang up now because the sooner I start driving the sooner I'll be there, so just... Hang on, okay?"

There was something under her voice. "What is it?"

"See you soon."

The dorm room was quiet except for the buzzing of the overhead lights and the sound of water running in the shower next door. My phone was warm in my hand, like somehow it was still connected to my best friend. *Hell or high water* was right. I had spent our childhood trying to protect her from her father, and when shit finally hit the fan with him in high school, I almost got arrested for trespassing while trying to help her move out of his house. When she lost her ability to cope with the world, I was there to hold her up. It was the way things had always been.

Turned out she could hold me up too.

I texted her to stop by the grocery and get boxes to pack in, but as I crutched around the dorm, my knee throbbing like a heartbeat, it turned out I had accumulated very few possessions in my three years there. All I had to show for it was a closet full of old but carefully maintained clothes, notebooks, my decrepit laptop that no longer held a charge, and a stack of photo albums. Three of them I'd brought from home. We hadn't been well off growing up, but Dad had always been sure to document the memories with hundreds of photographs, and I'd flip through them on nights when I got homesick—and I did get homesick. Not for my town and not for my state but for my family—for Anita and Jetta and Janie and Jules and Molly and Logan, but Dad most of all.

Jackson never knew I'd given Hesper an emergency key to the dorm years ago, but I had, and she managed to open the door and slip in so quietly my heart jumped up in my throat when the bedsprings creaked as she sank down beside me. She didn't say a word, just hooked her chin over my shoulder and watched as I turned the laminated pages containing all our history.

Hesper, standing by the community pool clapping gleefully while my youngest sister was a cannonball blur beyond the highest diving board. Hesper and me, asleep on the couch with shiny, pointed paper hats still strapped to our heads and unused party poppers in our hands. It was New Year's Eve, probably the last year we had a party together, because we were in high school in the photo, but I spent my senior New Year's Eve kissing a girl named Steph who hated Hesper. We broke up a few weeks later, and Hesper came over and popped popcorn and watched movies about robots with me—

"You've always taken care of me," I said softly, a revelation, "even when I didn't realize it."

"We've always taken care of each other. Is this...everything?"

"Yeah."

She started neatly packing clothes into a crumpled cardboard box. The albums were the next-to-last thing to go, then she sent me down the elevator with her keys to wait in Calamity while she folded up and packed my bed linens. The spark of anger I felt toward Coach Maze, had been feeling intermittently ever since my last game, flared to life again and I wanted to punch something. The thought of one terrible moment on a football field ruining the rest of my life was too much—and here I sat, while the girl I'd spent most of my life protecting tried to protect *me*. She was lugging my boxes down in the elevator. She was taking me into her home. And I had nothing to offer her in return—the only thing I had was *me*, and I was not enough.

She must have found the building's supervisors, because she came out with a dolly, four boxes containing my whole life stacked up so high I could only see her head poking out from behind them. I closed my eyes, rolling my medicine bottle between my hands like a talisman, and we rode together in silence for most of the way back to her place.

"I know it might seem...hopeless. Hard. Not worth it. But it *is* worth it, and things will be okay."

"You really think so, H?"

Her smile was half-hearted at best. "I don't know what I think. But I need someone to tell me those things, and nobody ever does. I thought it might help us both if I told them to you."

My best friend, but also an enigma. I had no idea that's what she had needed to hear.

"Together?" I held out my hand.

She clutched it, her grip surprisingly tight. "Together."

I turned up the music and she rolled down the windows and it was high school all over again, but this time I finally got it. The cold air and the soaring vocals and thumping bass drowned out the constant, screaming panic that had been eating me alive since I woke up in the hospital and realized everything had changed. I felt clean, blissfully empty. The only warmth in the Jeep was Hesper's hand, still clutching mine like I was a life preserver, though I was the one who felt like I was drowning.

I had been to her house a handful of times, but since there was a long drive between us, most of our interaction was through email and text messages. It was like seeing the room she grew up in, writ large. The kitchen was painted a bright and cheerful lilac, with half an iris border painted over the cabinets before she got distracted and never finished. The living room was eclectic: a big leather sofa, its surface worn down to softness from years of use; a recliner in one corner and a rocking chair in the other; a glass-topped table covered with a dozen printed articles with sentences highlighted in a rainbow of colors. Art covered the walls, but none of hers. It was like she valued the work of others more than she ever valued her own. Going to a museum with her was an almost religious experience.

"Welcome to my humble abode. What's mine is yours, etcetera, etcetera. The only off-limits room is that one." She pointed to a door under the stairs. "That's where I paint and it's my one space. When I'm in it, it's locked. When I'm not in it, I trust you not to snoop."

I saluted her, and she went out to Calamity to start unpacking. My crutches were still difficult, but I was improving; I grabbed a can of soda out of the fridge (diet, I noticed with a grimace) and hobbled to the living room, where I eased myself down on the couch. The older papers on her coffee table were from the library, articles she'd found to help students with papers. On top of those though, was a notebook filled with Hesper's weird, hybrid, half-cursive half-print writing. I could tell when she got excited or agitated—the words got harder to read. A spiral-bound book was opened next to it, a purple pen lying on top. A policy manual for the college she worked at and had graduated from.

"I'm looking for scholarships for you at Morrow, y'know." She stopped in the doorway behind me, two boxes balanced precariously in her arms.

"There won't be any."

"Not with that attitude there won't. I'll talk to the disability coordinator tomorrow and see what she can do for us."

It was hard to swallow past the emotion. *Us,* like she had taken my burden upon herself. I would never be able to repay her for this, for fighting for me and dragging me through it when I couldn't do it on my own.

"You're stronger than I ever gave you credit for, Hes."

Her smile was steel—hard and ice cold. "I'm really not, but fake it till you make it, right?" She tossed me the television remote and collapsed sideways into the recliner. She dangled her legs over the arm and tapped her pen against her mouth as she read.

"Do you want me to—"

"Shhhh."

"Unpack?" I finished, even though I couldn't with my damned leg.

"No, just sit there while I go over this." Her eyes never left the policy manual.

I turned on the television, flipped through the twelve channels she got by default, then shut it off again. She didn't seem to notice, and my mind began to churn. The ticking of the clock was too loud; Hesper was too quiet. I fidgeted as my worries ran away with me.

My dad had struggled to raise us; he worked two jobs and I had been mowing lawns to help him since I was twelve. Without college, I would end up in the same boat. To get a good job you needed a good education and experience. To get a good education and experience you had to have money, and at least a low-end job to build up savings. I was a former athlete; all I had in the books was a mid-level GPA and an injury that signaled the death knell of my promising future, maybe even NFL.

There had been scouts at that game. Things could have gone very differently.

"Oh, God," I groaned. "My life is over. I can't afford classes. I need to get a job. I can't."

She didn't look up, her scowl of concentration never shifting.

"H, are you even listening to me?"

"Shut up!" she shouted exultantly. "*Felix*. I've got it!"

"Got what?"

She flung the book at me, and I caught it instinctively.

"Read the policy manual. We're adults. We can do what we want. Nobody even has to know. We go to the courthouse, do some paperwork, and you can get on my insurance and get free tuition."

> *Tuition and fees shall be waived for all full-time employees and members of their immediate family. Members of the immediate family shall be defined as the spouse and dependents of full-time employees.*

The word "spouse" was circled in purple ink, so hard her pen had almost punched through the paper.

Holy *shit*.

Free tuition. And I could get on her insurance—so I could get my physical therapy, maybe reconstructive surgery. I might be able to play again someday. My NFL dreams were over, but I could coach a high school team or Morrow's junior college league.

I wouldn't have to give it up forever. Hope flared in my chest, then promptly went out.

Letting me crash on her couch until I figured a way out of this mess was one thing. *Marrying* me? It was too much to ask, even of my best friend. It would keep us both out of relationships for the year it would take me to finish my degree, label us both as divorcees for the rest of our lives.

"We could get an annulment after you graduate," she added quickly. "You'd get your degree, for free, and then it'd be like we were never even married. I mean, this sort of thing always works in movies. It seems like your best shot."

"You'd...do that for me?"

"Of course, you're my best friend. It'll be like the biggest, longest sleepover ever. Like, for a whole year! It'll be fine. BFFs and roomies." She flapped her hand. "So? What do you think?"

"I think, Hesper Elise Stalides, I would like to marry you."

"Then subsequently divorce me?" She grinned.

"We'll see."

She bounced across the room and pumped my hand up and down. "I believe we've got a deal—or rather, an engagement."

CHAPTER THREE

HESPER

LIVING WITH ANOTHER human is just like anything else: you can fall out of practice. Having Felix around the house was a change, and change was something I wasn't very good at. I had lived with myself and my strange moods and my silence since we had road-tripped across the country in Calamity as teenagers, and now there was another living breathing thing in the house that needed my attention. He had essentially lived solely in my phone for the last couple years; I'd forgotten what it was like to be around him.

It was, in a word, distracting.

I tore all my jackets out of the living room closet,

throwing them on top of the other things that had accumulated over the years: unopened boxes of tissues, cards of lightbulbs, a pair of earmuffs, boxes of sidewalk chalk, and half a dozen pairs of worn out and well-laundered gardening gloves. I hung his shirts in there, surprised to see some I remembered from high school.

He sat at the kitchen table making phone calls. We needed things we did not have; marriage was much more complicated than simply showing up at the courthouse, apparently. A marriage license had to be issued, and only if we presented the requisite documents; a three-day waiting period was in place before we could actually marry. Felix effortlessly pulled out his ID and social security card from his wallet. Unearthing my social security card was a bit more of a task, though a doable one. But we both needed our birth certificates. Neither of us had them. The waiting period was worse, because it gave me too much time to overthink and panic.

"You know this is usually the *least* stressful part of a wedding, right?" he said mildly while I scrolled through my phone.

"Fifty bucks for a replacement birth certificate! What kind of crap is that!"

"I'll ask my dad to fax mine over in the morning. I'm sure your mom has yours."

"She'll want to know why I want it, and you can be *sure* I'm not telling her!"

"Getting cold feet?" Felix teased.

But what he didn't understand was my anxiety didn't care whether I was excited or scared, it filled my brain with horrible thoughts and an overwhelming dread regardless. I felt like I was tricking him—like I was the one getting the better end of this deal and he didn't even realize it.

"If we're gonna do this—" I counted my breaths, which usually helped. "We've got to set some ground rules. You grew up with me. I'm sure it does not surprise you that I have—"

"Quirks?" he offered helpfully, and I smiled at his sweetness.

"Issues, Felix. I have issues. I freak out easily, I don't adapt well, and I have my moods. None of those are your fault, and if I'm having one of those days, I need you to remember that it will pass. That I am the problem, not you. I will do what I can to minimize those days, which means avoiding certain triggers by preparing for eventualities." I sat down across from him, my notebook between us. "I function best when things are predictable. Surprises and bickering tend to set me off. Some things will be off-limits, and you'll have to accept that."

It was hard to talk about myself like this—to admit I was faulty, that I had learned certain conditions made me more prone to mental health spirals. Like an old temperamental copy machine, there were tricks and loopholes and ways around my malfunctions. I knew those tricks but trusting someone else to remember and adhere to them seemed risky.

"Hes," he said patiently, reaching across the table and knotting our fingers together tightly, his thumb rubbing soothing circles against the back of my hand. "This is not a surprise to me, and there's nothing wrong with you. We can make this work. We'll be fine."

But there *was* something wrong with me. I didn't know

how to make him understand.

"We don't have to do this," Felix said gently, "it's completely understandable if you're uncomfortable—"

"No! I mean, I know we don't have to. But this is a symbiotic relationship. It's good for both of us."

"How is it good for you?" He raised an eyebrow. "To have a freeloader on your couch for a year, using your insurance and a tuition waiver from your place of employment?"

"You're my best friend. What helps you helps me."

There was more—more than I was willing to admit to him. I got the biggest benefit of all: companionship. I stood no chance of maintaining a real, functional relationship with anyone. This sham marriage was the only marriage I would ever have. I had always anticipated a long future alone; it was an inevitability.

Felix was my reprieve.

This was all an attempt to help him, of course. But it staved off the loneliness, at least for the year it took him to graduate. It benefited me as much or more than it benefited him. And I would not, could not, explain why.

He took my flimsy explanation and rolled with it. "Okay. New roommates can be scary, even when you've known them forever, because knowing someone and living with them are two entirely different things. What can I do to make this easier on you?"

Tears pricked my eyes. My mental health struggles weren't the only things that made it hard for me to function, made a relationship impossible. But it was too big, too much to share—even with Felix. So instead, I steeled myself, mustered the energy to fake normalcy, and drew a chart in my notebook.

"I fixate on things and worry, but the worst of it can be headed off with routine and consistent scheduling." I scrawled out my work hours, drawing a chart with days of the week. "Sundays are laundry and housework days. Thursdays are painting days."

"I'm not good for much right now," he said bitterly, jerking his head toward his leg, which was stretched out stiffly to the side, the bulky brace making his sweatpants bulge. "But I promise I'll help with household stuff, and I'm already looking for a job."

"Don't sweat it. Costs just as much to live here with one person as it does with two."

"I will not take advantage of you, and I *will* contribute my fair share."

"Whatever." I flapped my hand.

"What are we gonna do about rings?" Felix's cheeks and ears went pink. "If we're gonna convince Morrow—"

"Actually, I've got this." I held up a finger. "Give me a sec."

I darted upstairs to my bedroom and rummaged through my dresser drawer until I found what I was looking for: a green and blue enameled box that held my collection of pressed pennies and the few nice pieces of jewelry I owned. Buried at the bottom was a set of gold bands I had always intended to melt down and sell—the only remnants of my parents' failed marriage. I was pretty sure the "diamond" on the smaller ring was cubic zirconia; I couldn't imagine my father shelling out the dough for a real one.

I slid my mom's ring onto my finger. Fake or not, it twinkled prettily when I held it up to the light. It wasn't like rings carried memories; it couldn't be haunted or cursed like a house. Their tragedy wasn't imprinted into the metal. And it definitely wouldn't affect Felix and me. That was superstition, and a bad thought to latch on to.

Bad thoughts tended to take root in my mind and grow ugly thorns.

"These should work." My descent down the stairs was slower, more cautious. I dropped my father's ring in Felix's outstretched palm.

He remembered when my parents were married. I was sure he knew the significance of the rings that *definitely weren't omens*. My hands itched to draw him with the kitchen light hitting him strongly across the face, making him a study in shadows. I sent up a little prayer to whoever or whatever might be listening that I wasn't about to ruin his life and mine—that our friendship could come out the other side of the next year intact.

The ring was a little loose on him. My father's hands were bigger. I should have realized that—hadn't I seen them beat against the glass of my screen door back in Missouri, enormous and calloused and lined with malicious intent? *Pull it together, Hesper*. This had nothing to do with my father; the ring happened to belong to him once, but it had no bearing on our current situation.

But between the letter a couple of weeks back and this, I had no doubt nightmares would come knocking. Even though I'd gotten away from him, I would never be free. He lived in the darkest part of my heart, always.

"Ring sizers are pretty cheap. I'll pick one up next time I go shopping." I cringed. "Zach is going to freak out."

"I don't envy you at work in the morning," he muttered, his eyes focused on his phone. "We need witnesses, too, so have fun telling him you need him at the courthouse."

"Who will you have?"

"I'll make Jackson drive down here. He owes me for being an asshole and avoiding me once I got hurt." He grimaced. "And I'm gonna make him apologize to you, because that was out of line."

I instantly wanted to hide under the table, heat crawling all the way up to my scalp. I had lost my temper at Felix's roommate, because he'd hit a raw nerve. He hadn't meant any harm, but physical compliments made my skin crawl—because they always came with certain...expectations.

Expectations I would never be willing to meet.

"If he doesn't bring it up, I won't. Water under the bridge."

"That's fair. I still wish you all the best with Zach tomorrow. Try to convince him not to kill me before the big day, okay?"

Felix was teasing...mostly.

When we went to bed—he stretched out on the couch, insisting that even if I volunteered to swap and let him have the bed, his knee wasn't ready for my flight of stairs quite yet—I closed my door, sticking a towel underneath the crack that might let sound out into the hall and down the stairs. When I did have nightmares, they weren't quiet, but that morning I woke without a throat raw from screaming, and I didn't remember dreaming a single thing. Maybe having someone I trusted in the house with me kept them at bay.

Walking into the college library the next morning felt more like home than my actual house. It was familiar, comforting in its sameness, the tall stacks I could walk in my sleep and the faded blue-gray carpet with worn bare patches where too many students had trodden. I could close my eyes and walk you to almost any book in the collection.

It took Zach all of five minutes to notice the ring on my finger.

"Come over here," he demanded, leaning over the circulation desk while I darted by with a book truck, headed for the shelves.

This was necessary. He was the only person I could ask to be my witness...but I still wasn't ready. I folded my fingers into a fist, like that would somehow hide the band on the fourth finger of my left hand. My breath hitched. *Spit it out, Hesper.*

"It's kind of a funny story." I laughed weakly.

He was having none of it.

"You don't even date. Please tell me that isn't what I think it is." He wiggled his fingers, and I reluctantly put my hand across the counter for him to examine, though he maintained a respectful distance and didn't touch.

"It is, but it's not what you think—"

"I know you're scared of being alone, but you don't even like people touching you. You really think you're going to have a normal marriage?"

The reaction was instant, visceral, *painful*; my temper flared but I tamped it down. He had no idea the extent of the hurt he caused with those words, especially *normal marriage*. It implied what I had been struggling against for years: the idea that I was not normal, I was broken.

"I don't want a *normal marriage*," I snapped. "If you'd listen to me a minute, I'd explain!"

He glared, and I hunkered down against the counter in embarrassment. My volume had increased and no doubt everyone in the library, scattered at study tables and sitting in the computer lab, had heard my outburst.

"Okay, then. Explain this not-normal marriage to me." He made quotes in the air with his fingers.

"Remember my best friend with the ACL injury—"

"Oh my *God,* you can*not* be serious, Hesper!" he hissed, leaning across the counter. He seemed upset, but it was fear, not anger: I could see it on his face, hear it in his tone. "You know real life doesn't work like that, right? You'll end up getting hurt, and so will your friend. And it's dishonest. You're defrauding Morrow!" His voice was so low I had to lean in to hear him.

"I'm saving my best friend, and I don't need your permission to do it."

"I could turn you in for fraud."

"You won't."

His glare was intense, but neither of us budged. "I should."

"No, you shouldn't, and you know it. Sometimes life isn't fair, and it hasn't been for any of us—you or me or Felix. And if I can do just one thing to even the field a little, I'm going to do it. We've talked about it; we understand what we're doing." I stopped and regrouped, because that wasn't strictly the truth. I hadn't lied to Felix exactly; I had just omitted something that would have absolutely no bearing on him so long as we stayed within the lines of platonic friendship. "I won't be alone, and he'll get his degree, and everything will be fine. But I'm going to need help."

"You're gonna drag me into this," he groaned, but I smiled because I heard it—he was caving.

"Only for one day. I just need you to come to the

courthouse with us."

I sweet-talked the HR lady upstairs into making me a copy of my birth certificate—she had it on file—and Felix's dad faxed his to the library, where I snatched it up before anyone could see what it was. Over my lunch break I zipped across campus to pick up Felix to get our license. He had all our documentation in an envelope, and it felt like the beginning and the end of everything. I held it as he hauled himself up into Calamity, grunting when he moved his knee wrong, his face twisting in pain.

"What did you tell your dad you needed it for?"

"Insurance." He looked guilty. "Which is not, y'know, a lie."

"Today is just the license application. It takes three days to process."

Felix must have caught, and misinterpreted, my trepidation.

"Hesper, if you're having second thoughts, we absolutely do not have to go through with this—"

I couldn't shake the feeling I was tricking him into this, into thinking this was a selfless act on my part to help him. And I *did* want to help him, more than anything else in the world. He had dragged me through the worst days of my life, refusing to leave me behind even when I begged it of him. I would move heaven and earth for this boy.

"You don't want to marry me," I whispered. "Not even if it's fake. I'm a mess."

He sobered up immediately, and reached across the seat to slowly, carefully put his hand over mine. My chest tightened and I struggled to keep the tears out of my eyes—because he knew exactly what I needed, always. Because he never moved too fast and he respected me enough to keep his distance if that's what I wanted. Because I had been in love with him half my life, and he would get his degree and we would divorce and he would move on with his life, his girlfriends and eventually his wife would hate me, and I would never, ever tell him.

Because even if he felt the same way, I was too broken for it to ever work.

"Hey, now. Pull over."

I obeyed, and as soon as I put Calamity in park he reached over and scooted me right up against him.

"Listen to me. We don't have to do this if you don't want to. I will find another way to pay for school, and that's fine. But I want you to stop operating on the assumption there's something wrong with you, because there's not." He held up his hand when I started to interrupt. "Anxiety and depression are nothing to be ashamed of. Everyone has their problems. Anyone who says they don't is lying. You're my best friend, and nothing will ever change that."

Ah, but that wasn't the only thing wrong with me, and I wasn't brave enough to tell him the rest. Because so long as he wasn't in love with me, it didn't matter. He would never have to know.

I WOULD NEVER have told my mom what I was doing, because she would say it was unethical—and even with a fake marriage, she would be mad it wasn't taking place at a church and she wasn't invited. All the same, I wished she was there with me. I wasn't very good at femininity. Jackson had already picked Felix up, and I was in the house alone, so I stood in front of the mirror in the one dress I owned, chiffon and green as summer grass, trying to tame my wild hair into something vaguely presentable.

I knew it didn't matter to anyone else. I also knew it was the only wedding I'd ever have—it was a blessing, to even have this. My mom's ring felt heavy in my pocket as I finally gave up, wrestling my hair into a high ponytail and calling it quits. It was a beautiful fall morning, sunlight and cold, crisp air pouring through the open window and my favorite songs turned way up loud on my phone. I was about to buy myself a year of companionship with no strings attached. I was about to help Felix.

I was about to puke.

9:31 AM

Did you hear about the notebook who married a pencil?

9:31 AM

She finally found Mr. Write!

I groaned.

9:33 AM

I'd apologize but I'm not sorry. How often do I get to tell wedding puns?

I grabbed a white cardigan off the hook by the door and

headed for Calamity. Jackson had apologized to me without being prompted that morning, looking abashed—but either he didn't know the wedding was fake or he thought it was still funny to tie cans to the bumper of my Jeep and write *JUST MARRIED* on the back glass. Less cute was the crude attempt at a ball and chain in the corner. Either way, it would help sell the bit at Morrow when I returned to work, so I left it and climbed in. The engine turned over once, twice. I groaned, dropping my head against the steering wheel.

"Don't fail me now," I whispered. "We've got somewhere important to be."

The third time was the charm, and I pressed a fervent kiss to my fingers and patted Calamity's dashboard. The parking lot of the courthouse was pretty full, but I spotted Zach's familiar yellow car and Jackson's ancient white El Camino. I was the last one here, even though our appointment wasn't for another fifteen minutes.

Jackson whistled low between his teeth when he saw me, and Felix punched his arm, looking mortified—so maybe he did know the truth. This time I didn't take offense. I had gathered from Felix that his former roommate was just kind of an asshole, though his intentions were good for the most part—if immature.

"Classy drawing on my car."

"Thanks. Snazzy cardigan—a librarian even on your wedding day."

Zach sat in a spindly plastic chair on the opposite side of the ugly, white-tiled hall, pinning Felix with a glare.

"Be nice," I murmured, perching on the edge of the seat next to him.

Apparently, I wasn't quiet enough because Jackson grinned.

"He already threatened to, ah, relieve Felix here of some body parts if he hurts you." He smirked, and Felix covered his face with his hands—though the blush was still visible, all the way down his neck.

"I'm so glad our witnesses are having fun at our expense," I grumbled, standing up and kicking Jackson in the shin. "Switch me seats. Go sit in time out with Zach."

He cackled but obeyed, and I slid into his chair.

"You okay?" I whispered in Felix's ear, ignoring the way Zach and Jackson both leaned forward, trying to hear us. I clutched the certificate in my hands. It crumpled beneath my fingers, creasing and growing slightly damp with perspiration.

"Yeah, I'm fine. It's you I'm worried about."

"Like I said the other day—how is this any different from sleepovers we had as a kid? Except this time nobody can tell us not to drink too much soda, and we can eat cereal for dinner. There are a few perks to being grown-ups, y'know."

How many nights had I spent at his house growing up, the two of us ending up squished into the too-small love seat or sprawled out on threadbare blankets on the living room floor? A ton, right up until he discovered a keen interest in girls in high school. Everyone had noticed he was handsome, something he'd never quite grasped, but around junior or senior year the girls our age finally got bold enough to make their move, and he was always happy to oblige.

"Sit still," I ordered him, rummaging through my purse and finding a small notepad. I only had one pencil on hand, in a deep red called Scarlet Lake, but that was just fine.

I put down a few lines, just the general shape to give the idea of his face, and the hallway quietened down at once. Zach and Jackson disappeared from my peripheral vision. The panic and nausea were still there, but like a car alarm going off in the distance: they seemed external, *other*. They weren't part of me. My concentration funneled down to a perfect, fixed point, like the pencil was an outlet where all my fear spilled out, leaving me clean and empty.

Felix's hair was sticking up in the front, and it made him look like a boyband throwback sans gel. He was freshly shaven, making every line in his face clear and distinct, sharper and more defined; his stubble would be back within a few hours. He had on a newer pair of jeans with his brace on the outside, an ancient white button-up he wore to career day our junior year, and a blazer I swore I saw his dad in once or twice, gray and about fifteen years out of style. His smile was sweet, if a bit nervous.

I fixated on the way one side of his mouth turned up further than the other, the way his eyes crinkled at the corners.

"Felix Morlan and Hesper...Stay-lydes?"

"Stuh-*lee*-dess," I corrected, shoving my pad back in my purse while the world came crashing back to us. I stood up and held out my hand. "Got your ring?"

"Of course." But when he thought I wasn't looking, he patted the pocket of his jacket to be sure. He swapped with me, and we filed into the courtroom.

There wasn't a sound except birds singing outside the windows and the steady thump of Felix's crutches. His knuckles had gone white—he would never tell me, but I knew his pain medication had run out even though the pain itself had not.

I didn't know what I expected the judge to look like—perhaps a distinguished, unsmiling man with a white beard and stern eyes—but the woman who awaited us wore a friendly smile, her hair a cloud of tight curls and pink-framed glasses sitting on the end of her nose. Her demeanor instantly put me at ease, and she leaned over the bench, shaking our hands in turn.

"Ready to get this show on the road?"

I nodded, and so did Felix. Behind us, Jackson had grown somber for once. I looked over my shoulder and saw him with his hands knotted together in front of him, his head lowered as if in prayer.

"Friends, we have joined here today to share with Felix and Hesper an important moment in their lives. In their time together, they have seen their love and understanding of each other grow and blossom and now they have decided to live out the rest of their lives as one."

I closed my eyes, and Felix's hand found mine like a beacon in the dark, like he knew the guilt that was creeping into my heart...and maybe the terror and the secret thrill as well.

"Who supports this couple in their marriage?"

"I do," Jackson piped up.

Blood rushed in my ears. This was the moment of truth—whether Zach would put his disapproval of the whole situation aside and support me, not in what he thought was best for me, but in what I felt I needed to do.

"I do," Zach agreed with obvious reluctance, shifting from foot to foot uncomfortably.

Vows. Vows. Oh, shit. I'd kept mine as short and sweet as possible, but I scrambled through the words in my mind as Felix wobbled on his crutches, turning to me with that heartbreaker smile of his.

"Hesper, all my life you've been there for me. I promise I will always be there in return."

"Felix." I swallowed; he grabbed my elbow to steady me as I wobbled. *Don't throw up don't throw up don't throw up.* "You taught me to tie my shoes and I taught your sisters to swim. I can't imagine life without you; you've always been there, and helped me face every demon that has tried to take me down. I'll stand beside you, for as long as we both shall live."

"I give you this ring as a symbol of my affection and commitment to you." Felix slid my mom's ring onto my shaking left hand. I slid my father's onto his.

"By the power vested in me by the State of Pennsylvania, I now pronounce you husband and wife. You may now kiss the bride."

My mind went utterly blank but for the howling gale of horror. This was a very normal thing that happened in every wedding ceremony. Yet I had failed to anticipate it. And I loved Felix—that was without question—but I had never kissed anybody and hadn't planned on it either. To me, love had nothing to do with smashing your lips against another person's mouth, and frankly the idea of an open-mouthed kiss made me want to be sick. The germs. The *teeth*. I almost gagged.

He leaned forward but hesitated, realizing something was very wrong with me. I put my hand over my mouth, my skin burning with shame and embarrassment.

"I'm shy!" I blurted out. "Can we skip this part in public?"

Jackson howled with laughter, and Zach sighed. The judge looked nonplussed. It wasn't hurt in Felix's eyes—more like concern. I had shown my hand. If he didn't know how screwed up I was before, I had just given him the first indication. I wanted to run, to flee, to hop in Calamity and start driving and never look back.

But this was important. This was Felix's future, even if it meant he found out the truth about me. The least I could do was give him a chance at an education.

"What was that about?" Jackson burst out as soon as we hit the doors.

"Leave her alone, man!" Felix had gotten better on his crutches; he used his right one to *thwack* his friend across the back of the legs.

Zach pulled me away from their bickering, his enormous hands settled on my shoulders. There was nothing but worry, love, and concern in his eyes, and I wished for the millionth time he had been my real father, that I could cash in and do some cosmic exchange in the universe. He was more like a dad to me than any man I'd ever met.

"Hesper, if you're not prepared to talk about what happened back there, that's fine. But I want to make sure you're okay, and that I can trust that young man to be alone with you when it's clear you're not comfortable."

"I'm comfortable with him. I trust him. That's not the problem. The problem is *me*." I angrily scrubbed at my face, hoping he didn't see me brushing tears away.

He shook me a little, just enough to get me to look at him. "Listen up. You are never a problem, you hear me,

Hesper? Never. Anyone ever tells you you are, *they're* the problem."

"Can you adopt me?" I sniffed, balling my fists up in the sleeves of my cardigan.

"You're already my kid in the ways that matter." He let go of me. "Maybe it's time to go rescue your husband's friend though, before they both get arrested."

Felix had one arm locked around Jackson's neck, and they were both yelling on the courthouse lawn. He had managed to hold on to his left crutch, but his right lay discarded on the sidewalk.

"*Boys*!" I shouted, and if Jackson hadn't moved quick to catch him, Felix would have fallen. "Behave!"

I handed Felix his crutch.

"Let's go home."

We started toward Calamity. Jackson wolf-whistled behind us, and I held up my middle finger without turning to look at him.

"I'm gonna pretend I didn't see that!" Zach yelled, bending almost double to fold himself into his car. He beeped his horn once and peeled out of the parking lot.

As soon as we were alone in the car, Felix turned to me, suddenly serious.

"Are you okay?"

"I don't want to talk about it." I turned the key, watching Jackson's El Camino round the corner onto the highway.

"We have to, H. You kind of freaked out on me."

How much could I say?

How much was *too* much?

I took careful, even breaths, imagining a circle expanding and contracting in the same rhythm, a technique I'd picked up on the Internet when I'd been hyperventilating from an anxiety attack years ago. It worked, mostly.

"I don't like touching. You know this. This should not be a surprise." I headed home, the cans attached to my bumper clinking merrily behind us. "Kissing—even when it's just for show—is very uncomfortable for me and I don't like it."

"But you had a boyfriend in high school."

Breathe. Don't lose your temper. He's trying to understand.

"I did. And I did not kiss him, which is why we broke up."

"I don't understand."

I was humiliated. I wanted to take off the ring, hurl it at him, call the whole thing quits already.

"I was in it for the emotional connection. He wanted a physical connection that I didn't. Is it really so hard to believe?"

"If he laid a hand on you—" His voice was laced with anger, and I rolled my eyes.

"He didn't. The breakup was mutual. The point is, I'm uncomfortable with kissing no matter who you are or how much I care about you. I trust you with my life, Felix, but kissing is gross. Period."

When we made it home, I tried to hurry into the house, but Felix stopped me, blocking the door with his bulky frame. He leaned his crutches against the door and reached for me. He wrapped his arms around my middle, lifting and turning me so abruptly I let out an embarrassing squeak, before putting me down gently inside.

"I know it's not exactly carrying you over the threshold

but, y'know. Bum knee." He grinned.

I retreated into the cramped little room under the stairs where I painted—the closest thing I had to a studio. The closed space made me feel safe, and a window looked out on the little half-circle flower bed against the house. I tossed my cardigan into the corner and sat at my desk, pulling my headphones over my ears and letting everything else go away.

There was nothing but me and the blank canvas and the music that pulsed so close it felt like it lived inside me. I stopped existing as an awkward thing with so many faults and broken places that I would never be of value—I was a vessel, pouring magic out of my hands and paintbrush. I squeezed a tube of Payne's Grey onto my waxed paper palette, scraped Titanium White into it with my palette knife, and layered it on thick, a dark and moody sky full of clouds and a sense of turmoil. The closer I got to the horizon, the smoother I made the paint, thin and even, and I dipped my thumb in some lighter gray and skimmed it across the skyline.

That wasn't my favorite bit though. The best part was in the details. I moved the lamp that was clamped to the back of my desk slightly to get the best light and started working on the things that made it come to life. My brush was barely more than a few synthetic strands, so the dark strokes of the bridge in the distance over the water were thin and delicate. The metal rose and fell in arches that supported the weight as a train barreled across it.

I had started on the rocks on the shore, a dozen shades of gray mixed on my palette to cover the way they shifted in color when the lights and shadows hit them, when I heard a forceful knock on the door. I ripped my headphones off, but didn't unlock the door, scrambling instead for the roll of plastic wrap I used to keep my palette from drying when I wasn't working.

"Hes?" Felix called hesitantly. "You okay?"

"Fine!" I shouted, dropping my brushes in the jar of turpenoid I left sitting on the corner of my desk. Pigments were suspended in layers near the bottom, a timeline of all the shades I'd used before.

"How do you feel about dinner?"

I checked my phone. He had texted me several puns—his weird method of apology—that I had missed while I worked. My stomach rumbled, but that was no surprise. It was after six.

"Starving. Just a sec." I stood up, flipped my light off, and unlocked the door before emerging from my tiny little haven.

I sniffed; the rich aroma of toasted cashews and grilled chicken. Thai, from my favorite takeout place a few blocks away. Felix held a hand up.

"Close your eyes. I've got a surprise for you."

I obeyed and latched my fingers into the back of his shirt, letting him guide me as he crutched along quickly. Something soft brushed my arm and I jerked away, startled.

"It's okay," he reassured me quickly, his hand finding my elbow and easing me down to sit on the couch. "I just...wanted to make earlier up to you. You can look now."

When I glanced up through my lashes, I was utterly enchanted. He had stacked the kitchen chairs two high and draped sheets over them, running the tangle of Christmas lights I had stashed in the closet across them, making a twinkling ceiling over the couch. The glass of the coffee table was covered in takeout containers, and I smiled when I saw *no egg* written on the outside of one. Somehow, he still remembered how I ordered rice. Our little blanket-fort cave looked out on the TV, which was playing a movie about a goblin king that I'd loved so much as a kid, I'd worn out a VHS tape watching it.

It was difficult to swallow, to breathe, to think. What a lovely gesture.

"It's perfect."

"Hey hey hey!" He sounded a little panicky, tucking his crutches tighter under his arms and reaching out to wipe away the tears I hadn't realized were falling. "Don't cry! This was supposed to be a good thing!"

"It's a wonderful thing, Felix. I appreciate it very much."

"Well, I am your husband." He gave me a wink. "It's kind of my job to make you happy."

I settled onto the couch, expecting things to be awkward—but it was easy to fall back into Hesper-and-Felix, like we were kids again. I laughed at him while he tried to eat with chopsticks for a while before he finally gave up, dug into his paper takeout container with a fork, and shoveled rice and shrimp into his mouth. He stuck his tongue out when he realized I was eating my cashew pineapple fried rice very neatly with chopsticks.

He folded his arms behind his head, peering over at me, smiling so big his dimples disappeared into his cheeks.

"Obviously we're gonna be the talk of the town when we show up married at Morrow. What's our ship name?"

"Stop," I laughed, poking him in the ribs, but it didn't faze him.

"Fesper obviously doesn't work, it sounds too much like fester. Helix! Hes, that's our ship name! Worthy of fanfiction. Perfection."

"You haven't read fanfiction in years!"

"Nonsense. I love a good coffee shop AU." He settled his arm around me, refusing to let me budge when I moved to gather our boxes for the trash. "Just stay here. Relax. Watch the movie."

So I leaned into him, and that's what we did. It was just like being sixteen again, but so much more—a layer of meaning I was adding to it that he didn't intend. It was too easy to fall into this when I had fought against those feelings for years, knowing he would never, could never, reciprocate them. I couldn't even ask, because it wouldn't be fair. I was damaged goods. And if he was shocked I didn't want to kiss anyone, how would he feel when he knew the truth about me?

This, I thought sleepily, dangling my legs over the edge of the sofa and nuzzling deeper into Felix's shoulder, his arm warm and comforting and not too much—never too much, because he respected my boundaries. *This is the only kind of wedding night I ever wanted.*

CHAPTER FOUR

FELIX

I THOUGHT I understood everything about Hesper—and I understood a fair bit, that much was true. But I felt like I was creeping closer to some secret side of her she'd kept hidden away for all the years of our friendship. It was nothing short of terror in her eyes when I had leaned toward her at the courthouse; yet she obviously trusted me, because I had been stuck on the couch for hours, afraid to move and wake her up.

She'd slid down from my shoulder at some point, her head in my lap and her hand curled up on my knee. I brushed her bangs away from her forehead with my fingers as lightly as I could, and she only stirred a little. She knew my face better than I knew hers because I seldom got the chance to look at her before she shyly looked away. She had the advantage because she had spent our whole lives drawing me, sometimes when she knew I was looking and sometimes when she thought she was being sneaky about it. She was never as sly as she thought she was. I had fished more than one crumpled piece of paper out of the bin, failing to understand how her drawings always made me look extraordinary when I was so plain. I was no Jackson; I was no frat boy. But maybe she saw me a little bit different than everybody else. Maybe she drew how she felt, or how she remembered me on my very best day, instead of what her eyes actually saw.

No. Those are definitely not her feelings shining through on the paper. She had covered her mouth when I tried to kiss her, a clear sign of revulsion. I had started to think maybe she was growing into some feelings, but that wasn't how you acted when you wanted a relationship with someone. But this—movie nights on the couch, living in each other's orbits, cohabiting the same space—maybe this was enough. She made me happier than any of my girlfriends ever had, just by being my best friend.

I finally squirmed my way out from under her and managed to wedge a throw pillow under her head, needles of tingling pain shooting all the way down my good leg. My left one was swollen at the knee, a snarl of raised, red flesh where the wound was still healing. I reached for my brace, strapped it on, and gingerly sneaked toward the kitchen. It was funny—for all that Hesper was desperate to leave our hometown behind her, she kept her ibuprofen in the same cabinet her mom always did. I took three with a glass of room temperature tap water, afraid the sound of ice from the freezer would wake her.

Being married didn't feel as dishonest as I'd thought it might. Hesper was a much nicer roommate than Jackson; for one, I never felt like strangling her. She minded her space, and I minded mine. I flexed my knee, holding my breath against the pain and waiting for the medicine to kick in.

I was going to get better. I was going to walk—and someday, I'd do it without a limp.

THE NEXT MORNING, Hesper was gone from the couch by the time I woke up. In the night she had folded up the blankets and taken down the lights, putting them neatly on the table after clearing away the empty takeout containers and fortune cookie wrappers.

7:22 AM

Good morning, sunshine!

7:22 AM

What do you call an average potato?

7:23 AM

A common-tater!

7:23 AM

(Please don't divorce me before I graduate.)

I cocked my head, listening for a groan elsewhere in the house when she got my joke, but there was nothing but silence. Maybe she was still asleep; she had never been a morning person. I picked up her notebook off the table, scrawled a note so she wouldn't worry, and snapped my athletic pants down the sides. I rattled the door handle behind me, making sure the house was locked up tight before heading out.

Once I was out on the sidewalk, I shifted my crutches, stowing them under one arm and balancing hesitantly on my right leg. I tested my left foot. There was pain, but not as much as I was expecting—not as much as I was prepared for. It was unpleasant but endurable. The handful of physical therapy sessions I'd attended must have done some good; initially it had been unbearable. I had laid on an exam table, howling and cursing while the therapist pressed my knee flat then bent my leg again.

I counted my steps, limping heavily and dragging my left leg a bit but walking sans crutches for the first time since the accident. It wasn't the amount of progress I wanted, but it was a step in the right direction. I went back to the crutches forty-three steps down the road, before my leg could buckle, because if I fell there was no way I could get back up.

I heard it before I saw it—a vehicle driving at no more than a crawl behind me. My adrenaline spiked. Hesper's street was right across from Morrow's campus, patrolled by the college police, and—at least according to the Cleary Act Report they filed—generally very safe. A champagne-colored SUV rolled down its window and a tan, paunchy, older man leaned over the passenger seat, one arm resting against the steering wheel.

"Excuse me, did you just leave Hesper Stalides's house?"

Alarm bells. Panic. Because I didn't know this guy, and no telling what kind of creeps got overly familiar with her at the library, where she was obligated to help all patrons equally, regardless of how weird they were. I was surprised Zach hadn't thumped this guy; had he followed her home before? How did he know where she lived?

"Hesper Morlan, you mean." I held up my left hand, the gold band glinting in the morning sunlight. "She's my wife. How do you know her? You don't look familiar at all." I glowered at him.

"Old friend of the family. I tried to mail her a birthday card, but it got returned, and I was in the neighborhood, so..." He shrugged. "Shame I missed the wedding. Congratulations." He gave a halfhearted wave, rolled up his window, and zipped off, failing to stop at the red light down the street.

Missouri license plates.

Shit.

I tapped the license plate number into the notes app on my phone, turned around, and headed back to Hesper's house—*home*—as fast as I could. This was bad, so bad, *very very bad.* I knew what "family friend" meant. That man was sent by her piece of shit father; she had successfully stayed under the radar for three years and I had blown it.

I tucked my phone against my shoulder, but it rang and rang until Hesper's answering machine kicked in. I tried her home number—same thing. Calamity was sitting untouched in the driveway. I rested my hand on the hood—it was cold and still, so the engine hadn't been on. I hit the door at the closest I could come to a sprint, and it was still locked just the way I'd left it, but something was wrong. The air was too still. The TV was off, there were no coffee mugs on the counter, her stereo was silent.

"Hesper!" I shouted.

I checked the living room, the kitchen, the bathroom. Her painting room under the stairs was unlocked, but empty and dark. I sat on the bottom stair and went up the awkward, backwards way the physical therapist had shown me, pushing myself step by step with my good leg.

"Hesper Elise!" I bellowed, fear clutching at my lungs, making it hard to breathe.

I leaned against the wall, bracing myself as I made my slow, painful way down the hall without the crutches I'd abandoned at the bottom of the staircase. The end of the hall had an old, square, lead-lined stained glass window that light poured through. The door to the laundry room was open on the left. On the right, her door was closed, an old purple towel shoved in the crack between the wood and the carpet.

I knocked. "Hesper! You in there?"

A muffled noise, and I let out my breath in a great *whoosh*. I wiggled the door handle, yanking it open past the towel with a grunt. Her light was off, her curtains drawn, the green dress she'd worn to the courthouse thrown carelessly across the back of a wooden chair tucked into a desk. There was a human-sized lump under the black bedspread covered in neon stars, the slight telltale rise and fall indicating she was breathing.

"Hesper!"

"I'm fine."

The sound of her voice gave me chills. The gold SUV was

all but forgotten. I crossed the room in a few strides and sat down hard on the edge of her bed. She didn't move, didn't react like there was any outside stimulus at all. Her eyes were open, but vacant and heavy-lidded.

"Hesper. Talk to me."

She closed her eyes, burrowing further into the pillows. Tears had half-dried on her face at some point, but she wasn't crying when I ran my thumb along her cheekbone. She jerked back as if I'd slapped her though, and I dropped my hand like she'd burned me.

Every word she spoke seemed to take a monumental effort—like her voice took every ounce of her strength just to form simple sentences.

"I'm off work today. I'll be fine tomorrow."

"Talk to me, H. Did you...take something?" I began hunting around her bedside table, looking for anything that could explain her behavior—an empty pill bottle, a bottle of alcohol. There was nothing.

"Just my regular medicine." She tugged the covers up to her chin, closing her eyes. "Please go away, Felix."

If by *regular* she meant the antidepressants she had been on since high school, they clearly weren't doing their job.

"Some days are just harder than others." Her voice was so quiet I had to lean in to hear her. "I don't know why. Even if everything is fine, my brain *knows* it's fine, I can't stop this overwhelming..." Her hand spasmed, clutching the blanket tighter. "Dread. Doom. Like nothing matters and nothing will ever be okay. It will pass, because it always does. I'll go paint later. That usually helps."

"Can I stay?"

Tears started to well in her eyes, gathering in little drops on her lashes. "No."

"Is this my fault?"

"I just told you it wasn't."

"How often does this happen?" I waited, and she didn't answer. Either she was too exhausted to speak or she didn't want to tell me. "How long has it been like this? Have you tried a different dose? A different medicine?"

She closed her eyes, still crying for reasons I couldn't understand, wiping her face on the cuff of her flannel pajamas. I pulled my phone out and brought up a search engine to see what I could find.

Her breathing grew heavy, sleep claiming her, and it was almost a relief—at least asleep she wasn't hurting.

I didn't get it. I never had. She was *fine* yesterday, and this wasn't garden-variety sadness—this was something else entirely. While I would love to slay her dragons, this one existed only inside her, and that was somehow worse. This wasn't something I could ever protect her from. I stood; she didn't stir.

"I thought last night was...perfect," I whispered, but she slumbered on, or did a good job of pretending.

I didn't think her happiness was fake. So what triggered this? Was it something *I* did? I limped heavily to the other side of the bed and laid down as close to the edge as I could, giving her space. But I needed to be there, to hear her breathing. To make sure she was okay. My wound was physical; hers was emotional. At this point, I wasn't sure either of us would be okay again.

She slept most of the day, the light filtering in through the cracks in the curtains turning from clear and white to buttery gold as afternoon fell. I dozed off and on, and around five she finally stood up, trudged across the room, grabbed a pair of paint-stained sweats and a T-shirt from a pile, then padded quietly downstairs without a word.

The shower started up and I groaned, stretching my stiff, sore leg. It made dramatic popping noises that made me nervous. The trip back down the steps was easier, and I was relieved to see my crutches again. The sound of water from the bathroom continued for a long time. I pressed my ear against the door.

"What do you want for dinner?"

I was ravenous; my Thai food was long gone. Last night seemed like it was weeks ago, like today had dragged on and on forever.

"I'm not hungry. I have enough box tops saved for a free pizza if you want one though," she called out, and I was relieved to hear the change in her voice. She wasn't herself, but she was so much better than before.

I called one in, deliberately ordering it half-and-half—pepperoni and onions on mine, nothing but cheese and banana pepper rings on hers, because I would find a way to convince her to eat. Out of the corner of my eye I saw her sneak into the room under the stairs, a towel wrapped around her hair and her feet bare. Her eyes looked better, and I left her alone until the pizza arrived.

It turned out I didn't have to lure her out either; as soon as she smelled it, she elbowed past me to give the delivery driver a tip, snatched the box, and headed for the table.

"Thanks," she said simply, reaching for the cabinets to get out plates.

I ate my pizza the way God intended—using the crust as

a handle and devouring it from the tip-end first. She cut hers with a knife and a fork, methodically, into mostly equal pieces. I didn't tease her for it this time, and she called me on it.

"Stop walking on eggshells, Felix."

"I'm not!"

"You are." It wasn't accusatory, just a statement of fact. "And I understand. I just...get like this sometimes. And there's nothing to do but ride it out."

"That's not good, Hes."

"I know it's not." I knew she was feeling better because her temper flared, her cheeks growing pink. She ripped the towel off and shook her head, her damp hair sending drips all over the kitchen tile. "You think I *want* to feel this way? You think I *like* not being able to function? It sucks! My brain is a jerk sometimes, and I just need to sleep, shower, and practice self-care to reset. It took me a long time to learn how to deal with it, to head it off and shorten it and loosen its grip on me. So just...let me handle it. Okay?"

I held my hands up. I knew a surefire way to set her off was to tell her to calm down, so I left my arms in a position of surrender, then returned to my pizza.

She put her face in her hands. "I know that was out of line. I'm the worst."

"You are not the worst. Don't sweat it. I was just...scared." This was not like the depression she had faced growing up. This was bigger, outside and *other* and worse. Before, it had been a petulant house cat. Now it was a tiger, ready to tear her apart.

"Me too," she admitted quietly. "Bad ones can last for days; this one was shorter. I'm okay. Or, I'll be okay until the next one—and I'll survive it. I always do."

But what if, someday, she didn't? I didn't have the courage to ask.

WE SAT IN the parking lot the next morning in Calamity. Hesper's face was colorless with fear. All our documentation was tucked into a big manila envelope she clutched with both hands. I held two steaming travel cups full of coffee, mine black and hers pale with vanilla creamer, because the Jeep's cup holders were broken.

"I'm a horrible liar. They're going to know this is fake."

"Hes, it's not fake. We went through all the proper channels, all the red tape. What are they going to accuse us of? Not being in love with each other? That's not a requirement to be legally married."

She leaned forward and rested her forehead against the steering wheel.

"Zach threatened to turn us in. He won't. I know he won't. But..."

"Breathe. Everything is gonna be fine." I handed her the coffees while I got out.

"I'm not changing my name," she said abruptly, hopping out and slamming her door. "It's expensive, and it's not worth the hassle when we're just going to split after you graduate."

Her flippant disregard made me squirm. "Don't make it sound like that."

"Like what?" She stayed several strides ahead of me as we crossed the parking lot.

"Like one of us is going to get dumped."

"Of course not. There has to be real feelings involved for that, and—what did you say? Love isn't a requirement. This won't end our friendship. Nobody is getting dumped. We'll just...dissolve our legal ties."

And just like that, she was gone, whipping around a corner and vanishing down a hallway and I was left standing alone in the atrium of the Morrow College, wondering what I did wrong. Hesper was the epitome of *hot and cold*. She had leaned away when I tried to kiss her; she had come home and cuddled up next to me on the couch. She told me to leave her be when she was down; it had clearly hurt her feelings when I said love wasn't a requirement for marriage. Besides, it wasn't just me—she found kissing anyone, in her own words, *gross*. It left me feeling unsettled, like we were both bumbling around blindfolded in uncharted territory.

Which was ridiculous, because if I hadn't had some sort of emotional crisis over her in high school, or the past three years when we texted every single day, it was pretty obvious I wasn't in love with her. She was my best friend. She was frustrating and funny and whip-smart and talented, but everyone thought that about their friends. Right? I loved her, but I wasn't *in* love with her. And she had made it abundantly clear she wasn't in love with me—or anyone else either.

It didn't matter.

None of that mattered.

Eyes on the prize, and the objective was a degree. I was going to graduate debt-free and make life easier for my best friend and *screw relationships,* my last several had been disasters anyway.

"Excuse me." I leaned against the reception desk. "When does class registration begin?"

The guy behind the counter pushed his glasses up his nose and handed me a clipboard loaded with forms.

"Registration for spring started a few weeks ago, but plenty of classes still have open seats. Here's an application. When you're done filling it out, take it down the hall to the first door on your left."

Morrow was much smaller than Pearcy University. I was used to wide halls and little alcoves to study in and comfortable leather furniture. What Morrow lacked in size, it made up for in charm. It didn't have the cold, clinical air of stuffy academia. Everyone in the hall smiled at me, and yeah, maybe the carpet was worn, but instead of articles about wealthy alumni, the walls were covered in student artwork, framed like the college was as proud of it as they would be museum pieces. Bulletin boards lined either side, cluttered with colorful flyers for club activities, and beside the registrar where I was taking my application—

CAMPUS JOBS, big bubble letters tacked onto a faded orange paper background. *Maintenance assistant—must be eligible for financial aid.* Testing center monitor, same stipulation. Cafeteria cashier. I was about to give up and walk by when I saw one notice sticking out from under a few others, discolored where it had been exposed to light for too long.

Fitness Center Monitor. It wasn't a work-study job, but a twenty-eight hour per week contract job. That meant I could start right away. Cleaning exercise equipment, maintaining attendance logs, teaching people how to use the equipment safely—all things I could do with a bad knee. I could grab a few hours a week of strength-building exercises after I got off work, an extra chance to make the physical therapy go faster. I snatched it off the board.

Maybe things would work out for me after all.

CHAPTER FIVE

HESPER

4:19 PM

Why did the fruit go to the gym?

4:26 PM

Felix. I am begging you.

4:26 PM

No more puns.

4:27 PM

For the sake of the marriage.

4:29 PM

To get in some avo-cardio!

4:30 PM

I WANT A DIVORCE

It was only half a joke. I was a *mess*. This should only have been legal, but here I was, getting my feelings mixed up and hurt in the one-sided disaster I'd spent forever trying to avoid. Things had been fine, just fine, and then that stupid regionals game and that horrible injury and suddenly *both* our lives were falling apart—his because his career was over, mine because I had put my heart on the line to help him, knowing full well it would be disastrous.

4:35 PM

Don't you want to know why today's pun was gym-themed?

4:37 PM

NO

4:37 PM

I'm pretty sure I've got a job in the fitness center. We're COWORKERS now, Hes!

I could have wept with frustration. That meant there was nowhere, *nowhere* I could go where I wouldn't have to deal with my feelings. With his distinct *lack* thereof. Though when I had been going through my episode, in a half-asleep miserable haze, I felt every move of the mattress—he hadn't left me alone. Even though I was terrible company and unable to sit up or carry on a basic conversation, he stayed.

And if that wasn't love, what was? Maybe not the kind of love I wanted, but close enough. I had bought myself a whole year of it. A year of companionship and pizza and movie nights. A year of understanding and unconditional acceptance. That was something, at least. And at the end of that year?

I'd deal with it when it came.

Sometime over the past couple of weeks fall had slipped quietly into winter, and I bundled up in my comfortable old peacoat and earmuffs before heading out to Calamity. Felix was by the door waiting, his face lit up with a smile, his cheeks and nose red where he had apparently already been outside. He waggled his fingers in a greeting, the ring that tied us together catching the light. His crutches were tucked under one arm; he held out the other hand to me, and I took it, his big, warm hand comforting around mine.

I would have shaken him off, but newlyweds not holding hands would set off alarm bells. At least, that was my excuse.

He was limping less, I noted with satisfaction, and instead of a grim line of determination or pain, his mouth was turned up in a contagious grin.

"How did HR take it?"

"About as well as could be expected, given that nobody

here has ever laid eyeballs on you before and I've never so much as *mentioned* dating."

Instead of letting go after we trekked across the parking lot, he followed me to the driver's side, reached past me, and opened the door.

"Cheesy as always." I couldn't help the smile creeping onto my face, in spite of myself.

"I am *wounded*, H. Chivalry and cheese are two entirely different things."

I held a hand up irritably, grabbed the handle above the door, and pulled myself up into the driver's seat. "No cheese puns!"

He clutched his chest. "How could you! You know some of my best material is cheese-based."

"You don't have any best material. You don't even have any *good* material."

"You don't have to pretend. I know you secretly love my puns. Even the terrible ones are...*gouda* nuff—"

"Felix!"

He roared with laughter, like annoying me with terrible jokes was the funniest thing in the world.

"Are you...*feta* up with me?" He looked delighted.

"I will make you walk home!"

This sobered us both up immediately. It wasn't *the house*. It wasn't *my house*. It was home. Our home. Together. The most natural thing in the world.

WHEN I WALKED through the door, I saw it: the message light blinking on my answering machine. Why did I even have an answering machine? I grimaced and shoved a pink sticky note over the display so I couldn't see the accusatory flash of light, but I also didn't have to listen to it or delete it to make it go away. I could just...pretend it wasn't even there. Felix pestered me while I cooked dinner, mixing up batter and making waffles while he sat at the table with his chin propped up in his hand.

"I hear you can make crispy hashbrowns in a waffle iron," he said conversationally.

"Sounds messy."

"Sounds *delicious*."

The phone rang, and I tensed, but made no move to answer it. I felt his eyes on me, waiting.

"Want me to get that?" he finally asked on the fourth ring.

In the other room, the message machine beeped.

"No. Everyone who needs me has my cell."

"What if it's important?"

"If it's so important, why don't *you* listen to it?"

"Maybe I will."

"Fine!" I threw my hands up. "That's one less thing for me to freak out about. I hate answering machines. I should unplug mine. Nobody has anything so important to say they can't just text it to me."

His walk was slow and deliberate, but I felt a flash of pride. He still wore his brace, he still dragged his left leg, but he was walking. He was going to be okay, I *knew* it.

Felix hit play on the answering machine. I dropped the cup of batter I was holding at the voice that came over the speaker. Even when I wasn't in the same room with it, I knew it. I hadn't heard it in years, and here it was, back to rob me of the small slice of peace and sense of well-being I'd found here.

"I hear you're all grown up now. Married, and you didn't even invite your dear old dad. We have a lot to catch up on. Call me." *Click.*

"I need to meet this young man. Call me. We need to set up a meeting." *Click.*

"I have tried to give you your space, but this rebellious phase has got to end. Come back home. You're being so selfish. You're just like your mother." *Click.*

I raced for the living room and yanked the cord out of the wall, causing the house to fall silent. My next stop was the bathroom, and I barely managed to gather my hair back in my fist before I heaved into the toilet. Just the sound of my father's voice did this to me—left me feeling dreadfully empty and terrified and like I would never, ever escape. Felix's hands, cool and familiar, pressed a wet washrag to my face. It was cold and it felt wonderful, but a jagged sob tore out of me anyway.

I had been doing so good.

I thought I had really gotten away.

I was so stupid. He had ruined my life in Missouri, and I had no doubt he'd show up to ruin my life in Pennsylvania too.

Felix leaned against the sink and pulled me to him. I tried to bat him away, to shove at his chest.

"I'm gross. You don't want to do that." I didn't shove again though, putting my face on his shoulder and letting tears soak into his hooded sweatshirt.

"You have nothing to be afraid of. I've got you, Hesper. Always." He tightened his arms around me. "I always have, and I always will."

"He's gonna show up here." I sniffed, reaching for the box of tissues I kept on the vanity.

"I know." He hesitated. "I know this might be a stupid question, but why don't you get a stalking no-contact order on him?"

"It wouldn't do any good," I said bitterly. "It's just a piece of paper. He's a cop, and he thinks he's above the law. He always has. All he has to do is pal around with the local force and play the 'good old boy' card, and he'll get whatever he wants. Besides, an order of protection would mean he'd lose his state pension and they'd try to take his guns away. He'd die before he'd let that happen."

"Is that such a bad thing?"

"Not if he wouldn't take down a bunch of people with him."

I had seen his closet full of weapons, heard his rants about stockpiling ammunition because he was certain someday, inevitably, the government would try to take it away from him. He had three rifles hanging in a wooden rack over the desk in his home office, because "no man should be without a gun."

And if I tried to get any kind of official document to keep him away from me? That paranoia would no longer be unfounded. They *would* come for his guns.

Nobody would walk away.

"I forgot to tell you—I saw one of his lackeys driving down Eleventh yesterday. He stopped and asked about you. This is my fault."

I grabbed my toothbrush, desperate to wash the bitter acid out of my mouth.

"No. I got a letter from him a couple of weeks ago. I knew this was coming, I just..."

Didn't want to deal with it, so I did what I did best: pushed it to the back of my mind and kept living life like it hadn't happened. It was how I coped with nearly everything...by *not* coping. By weathering the storm of right-here-right-now, and then never looking back.

"He will not chase me out of my home. I won't go."

"I won't let him. If he wants to get at you, he'll have to get through me first."

I believed him. For all that he drove me up the wall sometimes, for all that we hurt each other now and then, it was something I knew with absolute certainty. We had each other's backs, always.

The smell of burning waffles sent me racing for the kitchen—the first batch was cold from sitting on the counter while I had my meltdown, and the second batch was so charred I just dumped it in the trash.

Felix slid a plate onto the table, looking at me expectantly.

"I can't. You go ahead." I sat at the table with a glass of ice water, my arm curled around my raw, aching stomach like somehow it would hold all my broken pieces in place.

Felix shoveled the waffles into his mouth, closing his eyes and sighing.

"If I had known you cooked, I'd have begged to be your roomie years ago." His smile didn't reach his eyes, but I wasn't surprised. Neither did mine.

"Of course I cook. What have you been doing for the last three years? Subsisting on cereal and ramen?"

"Don't knock ramen! It comes in a variety of flavors,

and it's quick and cheap."

"Well, as long as you're here, you're welcome to any and all meals."

I left the invitation open, wondering if it was too subtle for him to catch. We didn't *have* to annul after he graduated. We could keep this arrangement up. *I really am selfish.* I cringed. I'd happily keep him here to myself, though I was a dead-end future, not worth the investment. No kids, no intimacy—nothing to offer.

"Speaking of cooking, we missed Thanksgiving." He sighed.

"I don't celebrate that."

"What? Why not?"

"I'm plenty thankful the other 364 days. I don't need a day to be thankful. But it *is* totally acceptable to put up Christmas decorations."

"There's a *waffle* lot of cleanup to do—" He grinned, and I swatted him with a towel, scowling. "So why don't you put on some music and I'll do the dishes and we can start hanging lights and stuff?"

I left him to it, turning my cell volume all the way up and putting on an acoustic Christmas radio station while I jogged up the stairs to get the artificial tree out of the laundry room, where it spent ten or eleven months every year collecting dust in the closet by the dryer. The mixing bowl and plate and utensils clinked in the kitchen while I sat cross-legged on the floor, sorting branches based on the color of the tape wrapped around their stems, marveling at how quickly I had come down from my panic. It usually lasted for hours.

I wasn't back to normal, but I was functional. That was

a huge feat.

"Not a real one?" Felix asked from the door.

"I'm not murdering a tree just so it can die slowly in my living room. Also, I hate cleaning up the needles in the carpet."

He started rooting through a saggy cardboard box full of garlands and tangled strands of lights that played music when you flipped a switch near the plug, went over to the stairs and wound silver and blue tinsel around the rail, then layered the bulbs on top of it so they sparkled, casting tiny little reflections of light all over.

"You have a *lot* of Christmas decorations."

I wrestled the boughs of the tree into shape. "You know Christmas is my favorite."

He took the topper—an old, bristly silver star on a white plastic cone, covered in rainbow lights—and placed it on the top without even having to stretch. Tall people were the worst. I hummed along with "The Holly and the Ivy," carefully taking ornaments out of their tissue paper packaging and placing them strategically on the tree using little green metal hooks.

"Princess ballerinas. *Space Jam*. Spun glass hearts. Indiana Jones. Your taste is really...eclectic, isn't it?"

I stuck my tongue out. "Keep talking—I dare you. See if I cook you any breakfast tomorrow."

This was enough to make him behave, apparently. He had grown up seeing all these ornaments at my house, but I had never been allowed to hang them all at once—like some deranged decorator with wildly different tastes—because it looked "gaudy" and "tacky," according to my mom. I grabbed handfuls of iridescent tinsel icicles and draped them artfully across the plastic needles.

"I could make my mom's snickerdoodles," he offered tentatively.

I froze. He never talked about her. Sometimes, I wondered if he even really remembered her. The Morlan family was divided by a firm *before* and *after*. Before was filled with Mrs. Morlan's warm hugs that smelled like cinnamon, her gentle hands putting Band-Aids on our knees when we fell off our bikes, her habit of whipping up a batch of cookie dough for us to eat raw. After was filled with sorrow and pain, Mr. Morlan trying to be two people while his wife sat in jail for one moment of poor judgment.

Or rather, a lifetime of poor judgment that had finally caught up to her.

"I'd love that," I said softly.

"Even...after, me and my dad would always make them. It's just a Christmas thing." He shrugged. "I know it's only the end of November, but I figure since we're already in the spirit...right?"

"Right."

My family had always been nebulous. We existed close enough together that we could contact each other in case of emergency, but we all kept to ourselves. The Morlans were incredibly tightly knit. Felix called his dad every single night; his little sisters and brother thought he hung the moon. I had always sort of wished I *was* a Morlan, that I belonged somewhere. They had welcomed me into the fold even without any blood relation—Felix loved me, so by extension, they did too.

My phone buzzed, the music momentarily pausing before "I Saw Three Ships" resumed. Zach—who spelled out every word, which meant he wanted something. He ordinarily couldn't be bothered, even when he knew it pushed my buttons.

7:47 PM

Hey Hesper. How's married life treating you?

7:48 PM

Uh, fine? Why?

7:48 PM

Can't I take an interest in my favorite employee/adopted daughter?

7:49 PM

Of course you can.

7:49 PM

But you hate texting.

7:49 PM

Soooo what's the catch?

7:50 PM

Busted :(

7:52 PM

There is a thing

And if you did it for me

I would consider us even

7:53 PM

*Because you owe me for be-
ing a witness for a fraudu-
lent wedding right?*

7:53 PM

Are you...blackmailing me?

7:55 PM

*Come on, it's not that bad. I
just need you to take my spot
on the scholarship gala committee.*

I let out a little strangled noise of rage; Felix stuck his head around the corner, concern knitting his brow close.

"My boss is blackmailing me!"

"Like you wouldn't do anything he asked you to anyway."

"That's not the point!"

The oven beeped and he retreated again.

8:00 PM

*Meetings are Mondays and
Wednesdays at 1 PM*

8:01 PM

*Best of luck, THANK YOU
HESPER*

"Thanks for nothin'," I grumbled. I hated committees, and I *really* hated social gatherings. My phone vibrated again, and my inbox was flooded with forwarded emails from Zach about the gala committee.

He was on the decorating committee...which meant *I* was on the decorating committee. As jobs went, it wasn't a horrible one. I would probably be climbing ladders and arranging vases full of feathers and glittery artificial flowers, ironing tablecloths, and sprinkling star-shaped confetti in Morrow's colors all over. However, attendance at the event was required.

And it was *themed*. Good Lord.

I sidled into the kitchen, where Felix was sitting and waiting on his second batch of snickerdoodles to come out of the oven. One plate of hot cookies was already on the table, and I snatched one, breathing in deep and savoring the scent. It smelled like the Morlan house, more home than my own house had ever been growing up.

"Thank you." I took a bite, closing my eyes. "Oh my God, I forgot how amazing these were."

"They're the one thing I can bake." He got two mugs out of the cabinet and a carton of milk out of the fridge. "But with a recipe like this, who needs a bunch of fancy dishes?"

We filled our mugs with milk and toasted, devouring the entire first plate in a single sitting. He nudged his socked foot against mine. My phone vibrated again, and I wanted to fling it across the room until I saw it was a weather alert.

"*Snow!*" I shrieked so loud Felix almost dropped his drink.

"Geeze, Hes, speak up a little. Maybe the neighbors down the block didn't hear you."

He was smirking, trying to get a rise out of me, but nothing could spoil this. It was the first snow of the season. I grabbed my coat and jammed my boots on and ran out of the door. Nothing had accumulated yet, but it was magic, my breath coming out in small white puffs and falling flakes so big I could make out the delicate shapes of them. I held my arms out and twirled.

"You're gonna freeze out here!" Felix shouted from the doorway, leaning out on his crutches again.

The streetlamps illuminated tiny pools of light in the darkness, the points of snow shining. Nobody else was out in their yards or on the street. Everything was still, quiet, waiting for...something. Anything. I stuck out my tongue and let several fluffy clumps of snowflakes land on it.

I wanted every moment to feel like this—so full of potential, nothing pressing in on me or hovering over me, beautiful and silent. I pivoted on my toes one more time, my arms held out and my palms cupped upward, and caught Felix staring like he didn't know me. His gaze was intense and confusing, and my heart stuttered.

"I wish I had a snowball to throw at you!"

He smiled. "Maybe in the morning."

I jogged back to the door. He moved toward me rather than away and I wrapped my arms around him, struggling to keep us both from overbalancing. My face had been numb from the cold, but blood rushed to it, heating my cheeks as we stood in the open doorway, eyes wide, faces inches apart. Kissing was still germy, still gross, but I understood the appeal people must have seen in it. I certainly felt *something*, a tightness in my chest as I stared at his eyelashes, his cheekbones, his dimples, his perfect bowed lips. There was a little scar above his right eyebrow where he jumped out of a swing and landed badly when we were kids.

I don't know how long we stood there. If he had leaned forward, I might have been willing to give kissing a try. He moved slowly, deliberately, and whispered in my ear.

"What do you get when you cross a snowman and a vampire?"

I burst out in a fit of giggles, half relieved and half disappointed.

"Hey, don't laugh before the punch line!" He dropped his arms, stepping back. The spell was broken. The oven beeped insistently; the last batch of cookies ready. "Frostbite," he added, anticlimactically, and I shut the door, shaken at the intensity of...whatever it was that had just happened.

He took the tray out of the oven, and we settled on the couch, flipping off the light switch and letting the soft rainbow glow from the Christmas tree wash over us. His face was half in shadow but I knew it as well as—maybe better than—I knew my own.

"I have to decorate for the New Year's scholarship gala," I said glumly. "And I have to attend. It's from seven to ten on December 31st, and it's, uh...themed."

He raised an eyebrow. "Themed?"

"Midnight masquerade." I covered my face with my hands, cringing. "And it'll look very weird if I show up alone. So—do you think you could go? With me? To the gala?"

Excuse me while I crawl under the couch and never come back out. I was horrified. Could I have made that any more awkward?

"Of course," he agreed easily. "Just like our old New

Year's Eve parties, but with *costumes*. Which masked man do you want as an escort? Tuxedo Mask? Phantom of the Opera?"

I laughed, some tangled knot inside me easing. It wasn't weird, despite our tense moment on the threshold of the door—it was normal. It was just Hesper and Felix, the way it had always been. The way it would always be.

I stood up.

"Your knee will never heal right with you camping out on the couch. I have a king-sized bed, y'know—plenty of room. It's not like we haven't had sleepovers before."

"Are you sure you're comfortable with that? I don't mind. I'm just grateful you're letting me stay here."

"You aren't sleeping on my sofa for a year, Felix."

"Thanks." He stood up and stretched, then ambled over to the closet and dug through his laundry for the T-shirt and thin old pajama pants he slept in. "See you upstairs in a few."

I took the stairs two at a time, nervous without understanding why—other than the fact that I was almost always nervous about *something*. If it wasn't Felix, it would be something else. I locked the door, shucked my clothes and hastily shoved them in the hamper, changed into my pajamas. I unlocked it again when I heard his footsteps, slower and less even than they used to be, but he was improving, walking up the stairs on his own without his crutches or scooting up one step at a time. I pulled the covers up to my chin, acutely aware of every little noise and every inch of my skin. I had a *side* now. That was a thing.

Felix slipped inside, deliberately making noise so I wouldn't be startled, and crawled up beside me, a good two feet of space between us. I wished *this* was marriage; I wished just being close to someone was enough. But I was pretending, a kid playing house, faking like I knew how to be a grown-up. This was everything I wanted, with none of the expectations I *didn't*, but it wasn't fair to Felix. It wasn't what normal people wanted. So, in a year, once he graduated, I would let him go, knowing I would never have this again.

Outside, the snow continued to fall, and he turned on his side to watch it, facing me. Though he kept his distance, he reached out tentatively, slowly, like he was trying not to spook an easily frightened animal. I inched my fingers closer to his, the tips brushing, then he laced them together, warmth in the dark and the cold of the night.

"Good night, H."

"Good night, Felix."

His breathing dropped off quickly, slow and steady and even, his hand growing limp in mine as he slept. It didn't come so easily to me. I stayed awake for a long time, watching the snowflakes and wishing and hoping and praying and pining without even knowing, for sure, what it was that I wanted.

CHAPTER SIX

FELIX

LIFE MOVED, EVEN when I wanted it to stand still while I figured out what the heck was going on. Hesper stayed home, settled on the couch with a book, and I took Calamity, driving for the first time since my injury, to my final prescribed physical therapy session. I would be on Hesper's insurance soon, and she'd already looked into it—any future therapy would be covered by it, with a small co-pay due at each visit. But maybe I wouldn't need *too* many more sessions, because in my first week working at the fitness center, I spent every second I wasn't on the clock on a stationary bike, on an elliptical—anything to speed up my recovery.

"You've made astounding progress, Felix." Ava, my therapist, smiled as I showed off my range of motion. It felt strange to have my brace off, to have my knee exposed to open air. All I could imagine was it buckling the wrong way again, the sickening feeling of the joint and tendons popping loose. Once you suffered an injury like that, you were more prone to reinjury.

But I wanted to walk. And I wouldn't tell Ava this, or anyone else, but in a couple of weeks' time I wanted to be able to dance. I wanted to surprise Hesper, to sweep her up in my arms and twirl her while she laughed at the gala. I had never been to any party fancy enough to be called a gala, and I didn't know if dancing was even part of it, but it was a goal to work toward.

I had almost crossed a line the night it snowed, when Hesper ran outside and danced in the streetlight's glow and had, for a moment at least, acted like she felt a spark between us. I hadn't kissed her, but her eyes were wide and snow was stuck to her lashes and her lips were slightly parted like maybe it would have been okay to try. And did I want to? Did I want to kiss my best friend and screw everything up? This wasn't the obligatory, ceremonial kiss I expected to happen at the courthouse. This was organic, created in a moment neither of us expected.

Instead, I had told her a joke to set her at ease, because I didn't want to come on too strong. It had been the right thing to do. This was something I had always known about her: with Hesper, you had to move at a glacial pace. Was that something I was willing to do? Every girl I'd dated before hadn't thought twice—kissing them was as easy as breathing.

Oh my God. I am not kissing my best friend. What the hell is wrong with me?

I had been in love before, and it didn't feel like this. There was no wildfire of desperation between us. My judgment was clouded by how nice it was to have a routine with her—how I got to watch her try to muster outrage and struggle not to laugh when I punned at her; falling asleep holding hands; watching movies by the light of the Christmas tree, her legs draped across my lap and a bowl of popcorn between us.

"Something's got you worked up."

I jerked, realizing how much I had increased my pace on the bike, my leg throbbing. Ava's eyebrows were delicately arched, her red hair pulled back in a long, straight ponytail. She was pretty, friendly, funny. So why didn't I want to kiss *her*? I could have. I only wore my ring to Morrow. I was not in a relationship with Hesper.

Except the part where I kind of was. A one-sided one. Damnit.

"I guess I have to give you a clean bill of health. I'm very impressed at your work ethic."

"Guess the original verdict still stands—no more football?"

"No more contact sports, period. You could take up golf—it's a lot more challenging than you'd think, and it would be low-impact on your knee."

I followed Ava to the counter by the door, where she keyed something into the computer on the desk. She reached across and gave me a firm handshake and a genuine smile, and I should have given her my number, but I didn't, because she was wonderful but I already knew exactly what

I wanted and she wasn't it.

It used to baffle me why Hesper drove with the windows down, regardless of the temperature outside. Now it made sense. The clean, frigid air roared through the cab of the Jeep, so loud I didn't have room to think or worry. When I got home, I parked in the driveway and sat there for a long time.

3:02 PM

Did you hear about the guy who got hit in the head with a can of soda?

3:03 PM

He's lucky it was a SOFT DRINK!

3:08 PM

My first paycheck is burning a hole in my pocket. Can I take you out for lunch?

3:08 PM

Dinner?

3:10 PM

If there's a word for that weird time between breakfast and lunch, brunch, why isn't there one for between lunch and dinner?

3:15 PM

Linner?

3:18 PM

Lupper? Lunch and supper?

The longer she went without replying, the more my nagging worry turned into genuine fear. I remembered her motionless in bed, crying over things I didn't understand—things even *she* didn't seem to understand. How everything with her was fine right up until it wasn't.

I made the rounds through the rooms of the house, and when I got to the bedroom, it was empty. There was a tangle of blankets and a rumpled place in the shape of her body, but no Hesper. Her sketchbook was discarded on the floor, pencils scattered all over. The lamp was still on.

Whatever she had drawn was covered over with aggressive scribbles in thick, dark ink. Like she was unhappy with it, or like she didn't want anyone to see.

Back down the stairs, my knee screaming from the physical therapy and the cold weather, but I hardly noticed it. I yanked on the door handle to the room under the stairs, not sure what I'd find. It was locked. I beat on it with the flat of my palms, desperate to hear her voice. All I could imagine was her lying, despondent, on the other side in the tiny room where she painted. I yelled her name, and there was no response.

I found a bobby pin in the bathroom vanity cabinet, bent down, and wriggled it inside the lock, trying to move the tumblers. How many times had I sprung my siblings from locked rooms this way? Never had I picked a lock with such urgency. I fumbled and dropped the pin, picked it back up—how long had it been since I'd spoken to her last? But when I opened the door, she was just sitting at a desk, a large pair of old-fashioned headphones over her ears and music pouring out of them. She was inches from a canvas and her fingers were covered in oils where she had, apparently, been swirling shadows into the snowy landscape she was working on.

I wanted to appreciate her work, but I was too re-lieved—and pissed off. I stormed over to her and yanked her headphone cord out of her phone, which was in her pocket. No wonder she hadn't heard her text messages. Music filled the room and she turned around so fast she almost fell out of her chair, her eyes wide with terror. I felt bad for exactly one second when I realized she must have thought her dad had broken in, but it passed.

"What the hell, Hesper! You scared me to death!" I wanted to grab her, shake her, hold her close and protect her and never let her go.

"But I'm just painting." She looked dazed, puzzled, her eyes drifting back to her canvas. "Why are you so upset?"

"For Christ sake, *tell* me next time." I scooped her up into my arms, burying my face in her hair. "You could have been dead."

"But I'm healthy. There's no reason why..." Her hands fisted in the back of my shirt as comprehension dawned on her. "Felix, I suffer from depression, but if I felt suicidal, I would get help."

"Would you?" I asked pointedly.

She didn't pull away like I expected her to. "Yes. Some

days I don't want to be here anymore, but never enough to do anything about it. But I promise I'll leave a note next time—" She must have realized how that sounded because she quickly amended, "I'll let you know where I am and what I'm doing. I'm sorry."

I finally, reluctantly, turned her loose, stepping back and putting my hands in my pockets.

"Thanks for letting me borrow Calamity. I'll save up for an old junker of my own soon."

I'd had a car back in Missouri, but Pearcy's campus was big enough that I could walk everywhere, so I left it at home for Molly, who turned sixteen the year I moved away.

"Don't sweat it. You can take mine any time." She went back to her desk, folded plastic wrap over the waxed paper she had mixed paint on, and wiped a small, strangely shaped spatula clean on a stained yellow towel embroidered with some mail order art supply logo.

"So, this is where the magic happens." I looked around. The ceiling sloped down with the stairs above it; I could stand on the far side but would have to crouch by her desk.

Hesper checked her phone. "Yes—yes on dinner. If the invitation is still open. I'll meet you in the kitchen in a few."

I wasn't welcome in here. It stung. Several canvases were stacked against the wall under the window, where late afternoon light poured in, but she blocked them with her body, unwilling to let me see. She switched off the lamp on her desk, a big ugly rig with joints so she could move and position it however she needed. The walls were bare except for a few crumpled reference pictures on old copy paper, including an anatomically labeled skeletal hand, and a swath of fabric over her desk.

"What's this?" I trailed my fingers across it, a sheer purple, white, gray, and black flag pinned to the wall, like a backdrop for her work.

She turned around and her eyes narrowed and I could practically hear the *chink* of her armor coming up. "I don't want to talk about it."

"You can't just have a flag and say it doesn't mean something. If it didn't mean something, you wouldn't have it up."

"Remember how we said some things were off-limits?" She jerked the pushpins out of the wall, snatched the flag, and shoved it in a desk drawer. "This is one of them."

"Hes." I watched her shoulders drop when I said her name, but she didn't turn around. It took her a long time to decide to answer me.

"It's the asexuality pride flag."

"The *what*?"

"It's not that hard to understand, Felix. *A* means not. So. Not sexual. I'm not sexual. Asexuals—aces—can experience a range of attraction and desire, and honestly? I feel none of them. As a matter of fact, I'm sex repulsed. It's something that took me a long time to accept about myself, that I'm not broken, that there's not something wrong with me, that it's okay to want romance but not sex, that this is my *identity,* and I won't let your judgment take that away from me."

It all at once made sense and didn't. It fit with everything I'd ever known of her. She never dated anyone for long. Her dreams had never involved marriage or a family. But I couldn't wrap my brain around not wanting that—not wanting to be close to somebody. About what that meant for me. For *us.*

"Maybe you just haven't met the right..." She whirled around, her eyes blazing, and I wasn't familiar with this, this fierce and wild and undeniably *hurt* Hesper. I was used to her angry; this was something else. It was definitely the wrong thing to say.

"I've never been shot, but I know I don't want to be. It's not like it'd be better with a Winchester than a Glock or Smith and Wesson. Don't you *dare* assume I don't know myself well enough to make that call."

"I'm not!" I shouted, but my cheeks flushed because I *knew* she was right, that the error was mine, all mine.

"Do you know how hard I had to fight to come to terms with this about myself? To feel at peace with it, instead of ashamed?" She stormed from the tiny room and slammed the door so hard floorboards vibrated beneath my feet.

I heard another door slam elsewhere, and so I gingerly pulled open the drawer of her desk, removed the silky fabric of her flag, and pinned it back up. *This is fake this is fake this is fake*. But it wasn't. Whatever was between us hadn't been fake in a long time, maybe not ever, but this was uncharted territory. I tried to imagine actually dating her, knowing that if we were ever on the same page about our feelings and got married for real, my parents would never have biological grandchildren. I would never have my own kids to groan at my terrible jokes. *But Hesper would groan at them*. And strangely, that felt like enough. I could live with punning at her while she laughed in spite of herself for the rest of...well, forever. *If she ever speaks to me again*. If I hadn't ruined everything before I even gave it a chance.

She wasn't there to stop me, so I leaned in for a closer look at the canvas set into the easel on the desk. The paint had been applied thick, making swirls of texture. It depicted the dark-blue night, fading to lighter blue and a warm, soft yellow—pools of light under streetlamps. Shadows fell across the snow-covered ground. Two silhouettes stood between the lights, barely visible in the inky darkness, but I could make out one tall and one short, a boy and a girl, and the boy had a crutch under one arm and held the girl's hand with his other one, and it was *us*. The faces were invisible, but I knew it as sure as I knew my own name. She had been adding snowflakes by hand, each a raised dot of paint, probably left by her fingertips.

It was beautiful and it hurt because I never knew if I'd get a moment like that again.

I sneaked out to Calamity to make a phone call in privacy, because there was only one person I could talk to about this. One person who always knew what to do, even when I didn't. It took him less than two full rings to pick up, even though it was only two thirty in the afternoon in Missouri.

"Felix!" my dad cried joyfully, as if it had been years since we talked instead of, y'know, last night. "Ahead of schedule! Does this mean I won't get my goodnight call later?"

"Do you have a minute? I have...a big thing to talk about."

"For you, always. The shop's slow anyway. What's up? You okay?"

"Ugh." I slumped down in the seat. "I don't know. I guess."

"Doesn't sound okay. Tell me what's going on."

"Hesper."

Apparently, her name—or maybe the tone in which I

said it—was enough to tip him off. I had told him a little white lie, that I had gotten a scholarship for spring and we were roommates because she lived right across from campus. He had no idea the full extent of the mess I was in. That I married her first, and realized I was in love with her second. It was so backward.

"Ahhh, living together has opened your eyes, I'm guessing."

I closed my eyes and could almost see his wide grin. It seemed like I was the last to know about my own feelings.

"How did *you* know? You're not even here!"

"That coffee's been brewing a long time, son. So, what's the problem? You realize there's a thing between you. You just scared you'll ruin the friendship?"

"I'm afraid I already have."

"Explain." He sounded wary, and I supposed he had every right to. He considered Hesper a Morlan, if not in name or by blood then simply by association.

"I invaded her personal space—"

"Why?" he demanded.

"Because I was worried about her. Her dad's been harassing her, and she's been struggling. Emotionally." That didn't even begin to cover it, but that was her business and I didn't want to discuss it. If she wanted people to know, she'd tell them. "So I went into the room where she paints. It's the one room in the house I'm not supposed to go. And…I asked some questions, and when she confided in me, I said some insensitive things. She was embarrassed and angry."

"Spit it out, son."

"I…like her. I think she likes me. Or she did. But…" The

back of my neck grew hot. It wasn't an easy thing to talk about with anyone, even my dad. Maybe *especially* my dad. "There are things in a traditional relationship that she's very opposed to."

"Marriage? Felix, you can be in love with each other your whole lives without being married."

"Er. No." I cringed. I didn't know how to tell him that ship had already sailed. "Other...other things."

"Oh," he said awkwardly. How the hell had he ever had the talk with my sisters when neither of us could even say the word "sex" out loud? "Well, that's up to you, son. You know the expectations going in. That's not the only aspect of love. You can either accept what you'd be giving up, or not, but you have to be honest with her and with yourself."

"I was hoping for advice a little more concrete than *ask yourself if you can handle it.*"

"Well, you're not gonna get anything else because it's your life, and her life. I can't decide this for you. You two have to work it out for yourselves. Ask yourself if you'd rather be with her, knowing what you'd be missing, or with anyone else."

"That!" I yelled. "That's the kind of advice I needed."

I could date the most gorgeous girl in the world, one who was happy to engage in physical intimacy. But I wouldn't enjoy it, and I wouldn't love her.

Because she wasn't Hesper.

"That wasn't any advice at all. That was you figuring out what you wanted and whether you were willing to fight for it. Now that you know, go talk to her."

"I already hurt her. What am I supposed to do, go in there and confess my love to her? She'll never believe me."

"Then don't tell her. Show her through your actions. Prove you mean it so that when you say it, she *will* believe it because you've left no room for doubt."

"Thank you, Dad." I hesitated before asking him a question I'd always wondered but had never been brave enough to ask. "Do you still love Mom?"

"Of course I do."

"Even though you only see her across a prison table? Even after the accident?"

"Yes. Then, now, always. Your mother made some bad choices, but I've never stopped loving her and I never will."

"Okay."

"Call me tonight? I want to hear about the rest of your day later."

"Will do. Love you, Dad."

"Love ya too."

When I went back inside, I braced myself to apologize and deal with Hesper's anger. It was justified, after all. But her bedroom door was locked. I knocked, and there was nothing. I texted and heard her phone buzz inside, so at least I knew she was in there.

3:58 PM

H, this is ridiculous

3:58 PM

We live in the same house

3:59 PM

We can't avoid each other forever.

4:05 PM

I don't want to talk about it.

4:05 PM

GO AWAY.

>   **4:07 PM**
>
>   *No.*

I heard footsteps, but when I tried the door it was still locked.

"Just leave." Her voice was quiet, muffled. Not angry, just tired. "Please."

I pressed my forehead against the door. "C'mon. Give me a chance."

"If you don't leave now, you'll leave later. Everyone does eventually."

"I'm not going anywhere, H."

She made a derisive noise. "Okay."

"I mean it."

She made no move to open the door, but that was okay. That was fine. I had time to convince her of my sincerity. Time to convince myself that if this worked out, I'd be accepting a lifetime of celibacy.

>   **4:15 PM**
>
>   *What did the chickpea say*
>   *after he was a jerk?*

4:15 PM

"I FALAFEL about it."

4:17 PM

*I'm sorry, Hesper. I crossed
a line and I know it.*

The door was still closed at bedtime, so I resigned myself to another night on the couch. I lay awake in the dark for hours, alarmed at my restlessness; I'd gotten used to Hesper's hand in mine and the steady sound of her breathing. Without her, everything seemed too quiet. The last time I checked my phone it was three in the morning—when I finally stirred, I realized my battery had died in the night, so my alarm didn't go off.

I shoved two pieces of bread in the toaster, grabbed some clothes from the closet, and went to the bathroom to change. On my way back I snatched the dry toast and folded it up in a napkin, spotting a note on the table. Even mad at me, she was true to her word.

> *Walking to work. Need the fresh air. Take
> Calamity. -H*

Her keys lay on top of the paper. I could go to the fitness center and get an hour of exercises in on my knee before clocking in, or...I went outside, climbed up in Calamity, and headed away from campus. I had a stop to make.

CHAPTER SEVEN

HESPER

"IF HE HURT you, I'm going to kill him."

"Calm yourself, Zach."

He had seen the change in me as soon as I walked through the library's double doors that morning, a scarf wrapped around my neck and mouth and my cheeks pink from the cold. I tried not to act miserable, but apparently, I didn't do a very good job. Zach had hovered at my elbow all morning, making thinly veiled (and a few not-so-thinly-veiled) threats against Felix.

"I know he's your friend, but you don't owe him anything. Divorce the sucker. Make him pay for his own classes.

Charge him rent for living in your house too."

Living in my house? We've been sleeping in the same bed. But that was way more information than Zach needed to know. I snatched the holds list from the printer and retreated to the stacks to get away from the whole situation—the humiliating memory of last night in my moment of honesty, the anger that poured through me when Felix suggested I couldn't possibly know myself well enough to make my own decisions. How desperately I wanted to believe him when he said he wouldn't leave.

How I knew he would anyway, because at some point he'd want something from me I just couldn't give.

I sat with my legs pulled up to my chest on the floor of the history section because I knew there were no security cameras to catch me and grieved the loss of whatever had been blossoming between us. The door opened, but Zach spoke loudly enough that I knew he was helping the patron, so I stayed where I was, wrapping my arm around my knees and leaning my head back as tears gathered in my eyes and blurred all the book spines into a multicolored mass. The smell of books was comforting and familiar.

I heard the footsteps coming down the aisle too late to maintain my dignity. Before I could scramble to my feet, a bouquet of flowers was thrust into my lap. Stargazer lilies, carnations, roses. All my favorites. Before I could stop him—how would he ever stand back up with his knee in bad shape and in the narrow space between the bookshelves?—Felix lowered himself to the floor beside me.

I didn't want to talk to him.

I *desperately* wanted to talk to him.

My best friend. The man I had duped into marrying me,

with the excuse that it was beneficial to us both overpowering the realization that it wasn't actually fair to either of us. I clutched the bouquet and let the tears roll down my face and breathed in deep, relishing the scent. He sat inches away, our bodies lined up parallel but not touching, because even now, he knew that was not a thing he could do without asking permission first.

"I'm sorry," he said softly.

I leaned my head against his shoulder. "Me too. How are we going to fix this, Felix? How will things ever be okay again?"

"I'll tell you exactly how, and then the ball is in your court. Whatever you decide is fine by me. We can go right back to the way things were, and I can pretend I don't have feelings for you. We've been friends our whole lives, and I won't give that up if you don't love me." He held up his hand to prevent me from interrupting, because *of course I love you, you dumbass.* "But if you do, I think we should give this a shot. I know it's unconventional to marry someone and then ask them out on a date, but Hesper—will you go out with me? Please?"

"I don't think that's a good idea."

"Is it because you don't love me?"

"No," I sighed, and Felix cut his eyes toward the circulation desk, but Zach didn't come to shush us. "It's because you might think you're okay with it, but down the road you won't be, and it'll hurt us both."

"Aren't we both hurt now anyway?"

"I guess. Yeah. I suppose we are."

"Do you think it would hurt us any less to pretend to not love each other for the next year, then try to fake things normal again?"

"Ugh. All your points are valid." I hated to admit it. I didn't want him to be right.

I didn't want to think about the fact that he had laid the truth out there on the table: I loved him, and he loved me. It was too much to bear, but I couldn't deny it.

"So let's do this: let's take it slow. Super slow. And if at any point either of us are uncomfortable, we agree not to be one of those *let's be friends* couples who never talk to each other again. We agree to go back to exactly the way things were."

"You say you're fine with it now, but in a year, two years, five years—you'll eventually want something from me that I can't give. You'll resent me. I'll hate myself for it, because even though I've accepted it as part of myself, I won't be able to stand making you unhappy. We'll both end up miserable."

"Whoa, whoa, whoa." He held up both hands, dislodging me from his shoulder. "We're talking about a few dates to see how things go. Nobody said anything about sex."

"Everything is about sex, to everybody but me."

"Then give me a chance to prove to you it won't be like that. That's all I'm asking for—that we give this a fair chance. Because, between you and me? I think it'll work out just fine." He swallowed, his Adam's apple bobbing nervously. "Because when two people love each other, things work themselves out, right?"

Things almost never worked out. My parents ended up divorced, my mom so bitter she never remarried. Felix's own mother had been sent to prison for a DUI hit-and-run, leaving his father to raise all their kids and pine after her for years while the world passed him by. Every bit of evidence in our lives was contrary to his assertion.

But I wanted to believe it. I wanted to think there was a chance for us.

"You still can't kiss me until I'm ready."

"That's fine."

"And I will literally never want to have sex. Hell will freeze solid first."

"Also fine."

"Then I guess, Felix Morlan, we'll go on a date."

"OhthankGod," he whooshed out in a single breath, covering his face with his hands. "Do you know how nervous I was?"

I laughed. I couldn't help myself. "Why? It's just me."

"That's why. It's *you*." His gaze was intense, and I clutched the bouquet closer, embarrassed. "Not some random girl at the gym or at a football game or in a class who wants to cheat off my tests. It's *you*, Hesper. You're special to me. And if I fuck this up, I'll never get a chance to make it right again, but it's a risk I'm willing to take. Because you're worth it."

"*Hey*. Language."

We both looked up to see Zach towering over us at the end of the aisle, his hands on his hips, but his expression was soft in spite of himself. He reached down to help Felix to his feet, but he wasn't so quiet when he leaned in and whispered that I couldn't hear him.

"If you hurt my library daughter, you will be sorry for the rest of your life, you hear me?"

"Yes, sir," Felix murmured, his eyes wide and a little scared, probably because he knew Zach would make good on his promise. He flinched, one moment of pain from his knee, before limping down the aisle.

I wasn't ready to kiss him yet. I might have been that night in the snow, but we had backslid since then; it would take time to get back there, time I was willing to invest. I hoped Felix was willing too. I unfolded myself from my crunched-up position on the floor, stood, and thrust my bouquet at Zach to hold, and I threw my arms around Felix. His arms were tight around me, and I held on to him like I was drowning. I didn't usually like physical contact, but this was *Felix*. This was different. He had spent more than a decade earning that trust with me.

If he didn't break it.

"Thank you for giving me a chance, H," he whispered.

Zach swatted him with a newspaper from the periodicals section. "Get out of my library and stop distracting my employee."

I smiled, and so did Felix, and so did Zach, though he tried to hide it. And I felt like maybe things would be okay.

THE BAD NEWS: I hated gala committee meetings. The good news: the semester was almost over so there were fewer students milling around the halls, and I finally got to start decorating. The gala was held every year in the conference rooms off the atrium—spacious areas that could be subdivided by movable partitions.

I hung black sheets of fabric on the walls, gathered tulle into bunches and made swags from them. In the middle of each I pinned a flower I'd made from ribbons, surrounded by a cluster of midnight-blue and emerald-green feathers I'd coated with iridescent pearl spray. Another committee member, Jasmine, stood back and admired my work.

"Why haven't you ever been in on the gala before? That looks fantastic."

"Because the gala is a party, and y'know who attends parties? People. I don't do so well with people. The more of them there are, the less energy I have to go around."

"But it's a *fun* party." She held the ladder for me as I climbed down.

There was glitter everywhere—on my hands, up my arms, in my hair.

"There's no such thing as a fun party."

She looked at me like I'd grown a second head, then wandered off. Social gatherings were a recipe for disaster. There were so many people, and they were so crowded, and honestly if I could reach out and touch someone, they were too close to me. I couldn't handle the noise level, the crush of bodies, the expectation of vapid small talk that inevitably turned into prying questions.

But things would be different this time. There was a lot of experience and medication under the bridge since high school, since the disastrous school dances, especially prom. While I still had my moments, I felt more equipped to handle it. Like I could stay afloat in the tide of partygoers instead of drowning in it. My coping skills had gotten better, because I'd gotten help.

I could handle this.

(If I repeated it enough to myself, it might come true.)

I helped the maintenance guys roll out the big, circular tables we usually kept in storage and arranged them according to Jasmine's neat little diagram. She was into the logistics of the thing, and I was into the aesthetics; despite our differences, we actually made a pretty good team. I was just glad I wasn't on door duty, selling tickets and marking attendees off a list.

Jasmine brought me a compact ironing board and we sat down together while I pressed the tablecloths and she worked on a list, making bullet points and prioritizing to-do items like the organizational champ I would never be. Her notebook was even color coded. Big event planning was never my strong suit.

"Have you thought about what you're gonna wear to the gala?" She rested her chin in her hands, her dark eyes mischievous.

"Ugh."

"You can*not* tell me you're not excited by the opportunity to dress up. Not liking people, I get that. But even if you hated prom, the best part was dressing up and feeling like a princess."

"Maybe *you* looked like a princess. *I* looked like a scullery maid."

She laughed. "Nonsense."

"I actually went to prom with my husband." It felt weird to say, even if it was the truth. "And I was so freaked out I spent most of the night trying not to hyperventilate in the bathroom. But he stood right outside and waited and missed the whole dance."

"Sounds like a keeper."

"Yeah. Minus the puns."

"The *puns*?" She sounded delighted. "Hesper, how did you keep this man under wraps for so long?"

"Why don't we talk about dresses again? Clothes are

less terrifying than interpersonal relationships."

"You're a strange one." Jasmine smiled though and obliged. "I don't have a date, so I'm rockin' it solo. I have an orange dress I've been saving for a special occasion. Who knows? Maybe it'll help me land a catch."

"I think I have...a dress...in my closet," I offered tentatively. My mind went to the green dress I'd worn to the courthouse. I'd left it balled up on the floor; had I even seen it since?

"One? Singular?"

"Yeah? Is that a problem?"

"No! No, I just... Do you want to go shopping?"

Oh no, how do I people? How do normal humans interact? Abort mission, operation pretend-to-be-normal has failed. I had been a student at Morrow for two years, had been a student worker then an actual employee in the library for the entirety of my time in Pennsylvania, but other than Zach I hadn't made any new friends. I could barely maintain the relationships I had; how could I possibly balance new ones too? Jasmine Miller had been teaching math at Morrow since before I got here, but until I got stuck with the gala committee, she had never even deigned to say hello.

"You okay, Hesper?"

"Yes! Yes to both, I mean. I'm okay, and also, shopping sounds nice. Shopping. A thing normal people do. For a dress. For a party I don't actually want to go to."

She cackled, drumming her long, perfectly maintained nails on the table. "It won't be so bad—especially once we find you a dress. Let's go tonight. If we wait, we might not find anything cute in your size."

That was actually a very good idea. If I gave myself time

to brood about social interaction, I usually got freaked out and canceled. Jasmine took several completed tablecloths and spread them neatly before putting a small, round mirror in the center of each one, and I followed behind her, placing a clear glass bowl filled with coils of fairy lights and more iridescent feathers on the mirrors.

4:57 PM

Going shopping with a friend. I'll let you know when I'm on my way back.

4:59 PM

Y'know what they say. Once you've seen one shopping center, you've seen a mall ;D

"See?" I thrust my phone at Jasmine. "This is the kind of nonsense I put up with."

"You weren't kidding about the puns." She tried, and failed, to hide a smile.

After we finished with the tables, I followed her out to her car, and she blasted the heat as we sat shivering in the December cold. I pulled my phone out again to text Zach to water my flowers—I'd put them in a vase on my desk—and saw I had missed seven calls. *Seven.* A number from Missouri. A number I knew well. My home phone had been compromised, one of his cronies had been spying on my street, and now he knew my cell. I blocked the number with shaking fingers, but it wouldn't change a thing. He'd call from another number, alter it so it looked like someone I trusted. Because my father never quit when he had his mind set on something, and he had never accepted losing control over me. He wouldn't stop until he had me back under his thumb.

"Are you sure you're up for this? We can go this weekend."

I had forgotten Jasmine was even there. She leaned toward me, her black hair falling in a perfectly straight curtain over her shoulders, her eyebrows scrunched up in concern.

"I'm fine." It was a lie I told so often, I almost believed it myself.

She chattered about the instructional department drama (apparently there was a feud going between the biology teacher and the math and science department chair) and her ex-girlfriend (who she was still pining for and had plans to win back over in the aforementioned orange dress, since she'd seen her name—without a plus-one—on the list of ticket holders). We strolled across the mall parking lot, and she tried to get me to spill more details about Felix.

"So, how long have you been together? Was it before or after you were taken in by his terrible jokes?"

I pushed open the double doors. I didn't even know where the formalwear section *was*. "Friends? Our whole lives. As for when I fell in love with him..." I hesitated, trying to pinpoint that first, soul-crushing moment I knew, when I didn't have a name for my identity yet but understood what I did and didn't want. When I thought it was impossible for him to love me back. "Is it cheesy to say I think I've always been in love with him?"

She squealed, smacking my arm, and I drew back, alarmed. "Oh my God, Hesper! He's the guy who works at the fitness center, right?" She fanned herself with her hand. "You're so lucky."

"Yes, I am." I tamped down a flare of jealousy. I'd been keeping it under control for years, feigning happiness for him and all the girls he dated before and consoling him, feeling guilty at my own relief, when they broke up. I held out my hand, admiring my mom's ring. "We had a small ceremony earlier this year."

This was not exactly a lie, even if *earlier this year* was, in fact, a month ago and we had yet to go on a proper date. Jasmine went through the racks of dresses, narrowing her eyes at me and tossing dresses on hangers my way. I fumbled but caught them.

"You can't expect me to try all these on!"

"Why not?"

"I thought it would just be, 'oh, this looks nice' and I'd buy one and that'd be the end of it. Besides, I didn't even tell you my size—"

"Twelve?"

I stared, confused. "How did you—"

She winked. "It's part of my superpower. You might be a good decorator, but I'm a fashionista. I know clothes and body types. Trust me, all of those will look amazing on you."

I grumbled but trundled into the dressing room with a heap of things to try on.

"You have to show me each one! Come out and do a twirl for me," Jasmine called from outside.

"Stop being so bossy!"

"C'mon. You'll hate everything and won't let me see,

and then you'll miss the most fantastic dress 'cause you're self-conscious. I'm like, your fairy godmother. Let me do my thing, okay?"

"I don't even know how to put some of these on," I complained.

"Get creative. You got this, girl."

"This looks like a wedding dress." I heaved one over the door, hoping she'd catch it.

"Stop being so picky."

I tried on dress after dress—a gorgeous red one with an unfortunate, scandalous split that went up to my thigh ("You can totally pull it off," Jasmine insisted, before I reminded her Morrow was a college and there was in fact a dress code); a dowdy, plain one in pale yellow with a high neckline, three-quarter length sleeves and a bell skirt that ended just under my knees (I loved it, but Jasmine vetoed); a burgundy sheath that made it impossible to walk, so when I went out to show Jasmine I had to waddle like a penguin. I still had a bunch of dresses in my pile of potentials, but as soon as I laid my hands on the dusty lilac dress I knew it was the one. Maybe this was what most women felt like picking out their wedding dresses, because I'd heard of this—this instant intuition of *this is it*.

I walked out of the dressing room and Jasmine whistled, her eyebrows shooting up. It was shimmery, the bodice gathered down the middle and dipped to a point where the skirt flared out, made from hundreds of loose handkerchiefs of fabric in every shade of purple imaginable, each varied in length by a couple of inches and coming to beautiful, lace-edged little points. I twirled; it spun around me. It was magic. I loved it.

"See, aren't you a *little* bit excited about the gala now?"

I turned around. The back was a silver-ribboned corset. When she reached to help me tie it, I skittered back into the dressing room.

"I don't need to tie it. I know this is the one." I looked at the price tag and cringed. "Yikes. A hundred and fifty dollars for a dress I'm gonna wear once? I might as well donate the cash to the gala and just not attend."

"How did that dress make you feel, Hesper?"

I paused in the process of stepping out of it and shimmying back into my slacks and sweater. "It was nice."

"If you buy the dress, will you be short on grocery money, or bills?"

"No."

"Did it make you feel like a princess?"

"Yes."

"Then buy it."

So I did, trying not to think of all the textbooks that much money would buy as the cashier rang me up. All around us, last-minute Christmas shoppers bustled around arguing with each other and marking items off lists, and I was grateful when the cold nighttime air hit my face, refreshing and silent, when we headed back to Jasmine's car.

My phone vibrated rapidly, and I answered it immediately because it was Felix, and he only called in emergencies. My pulse pounded in my ears. When Jasmine asked what was wrong, I held up my hand, already struggling to hear on the phone.

"Hesper?"

"Yeah, it's me. Are you okay?"

"Do you keep a key outside?"

"In case I lock myself out. It's in a magnetic box stuck to the top of the screen door. Why?"

"Someone broke in, but there were no signs of forced entry."

A whirlwind of screaming terror. "Tell me you're okay, Felix." I covered my other ear with my hand to drown out Jasmine's concerned questions.

"I'm fine, but the guy—it was the guy in the gold SUV. The one who asked about you. He tried taking some stuff, but I scared him off when I got home." I heard police sirens in the background and voices talking over each other.

"Tell me what he looked like."

I leaned forward in the seat, my stomach rolling, my heart racing. When he described him, I recognized him instantly—a man who worked for my dad, one of his skeezy henchmen named Randy. Any time he needed anything done but didn't want to get his hands dirty, he sent Randy, and in all likelihood he had told Randy to catch us inside. Because he knew that would make us afraid, and fear was his game.

I felt like I was caught in a trap, and the harder I struggled to get away, the tighter it became until I was choking and escape was impossible. I should have known changing locations wouldn't be enough to stop him. *Nothing* would stop him. But this was somehow worse, because now I'd dragged Felix down with me, and my father was closing in.

CHAPTER EIGHT

FELIX

HESPER'S TEETH WERE chattering when her friend dropped her off. I met them in the driveway, and the girl in the driver's seat hung out of the window.

"Take good care of her!" she ordered, pointing at me. "We'll never find a decorator to replace her. My name is Jasmine Miller—I put my number in her phone. If she needs anything, you call, okay?"

I wanted to say that I was her husband, that I could take care of her, but honestly, every person watching Hesper's back was a good thing. I knew her father, I knew what was at stake, and I knew he wouldn't stop until he got what he wanted—what he felt was owed to him. Jasmine didn't back out of the driveway until we were inside and the door was locked, her headlights vanishing into the night.

I gently pried the shopping bag out of Hesper's stiff fingers. It was like she was a crashed computer program, and I didn't know how to reboot her. She sat down at the table and I went from room to room, methodically checking each window to make sure it was locked, checking each closet to make sure there was nobody in it.

The police had checked, but her dad was a cop too. How many times had he abused his power to terrorize her—pull her over when she was driving back roads alone, follow her to and from her crappy fast-food job in high school? Not all officers of the law were the good guys—and they had a tendency to protect their own. All he would have to do is lean in conspiratorially and go, "You know how rebellious young kids can be. I'm just trying to check in on my daughter since she won't answer my calls," and instantly, all inquiries against him would be dropped. It was the way things had always been.

Her dad was a piece of work, but somehow, he always came out on top—except when Hesper fled Missouri. He probably could have dealt with losing *her*—he never wanted a daughter anyway—but it was the principle of the thing.

It was the fact that he had lost, and he *hated* to lose.

"I'm sorry I got you mixed up in this."

"This has been going on for years. Even if I was still at Pearcy, lived an hour away, never even realized—" that I was in love with her? It felt like too much, like I was pressuring her. "I'd still be right here beside you. Because you watch out for me, and I watch out for you. It's what makes us...*us*." I reached for the last time she had gone through one of her episodes, grasping for what worked, what made her feel more like herself. "Go get a shower. It'll clear your head and make you feel better. I'll call in Thai. Everything will be fine."

"Thank you." She stood up, wobbling slightly, then leaned forward and kissed my cheek before retreating to the bathroom and slamming the door.

I put my hand to my face, expecting the shape of her lips to be branded there, but there was nothing, no proof of the progress we were making. I had been a football star, a prom king, a popular kid—I'd been on plenty of dates and kissed a lot of girls. But none of them felt as important as this one, as significant.

If Jackson was there, he'd slap my shoulder and say, "You've got it bad, dude." And he'd be right. I tipped the delivery guy and laid our food out on the living room coffee table. When Hesper emerged, she was barefoot, wearing her soft, faded old pajamas, her damp hair hanging in waves down her back.

I patted the spot on the sofa next to me, where she sat cross-legged and smiled at my attempt to use chopsticks. I was still no great shakes, but I had improved miles since the night of our wedding. She leaned against me and ate her rice and cashews and caught me staring once or twice.

"Do I have something on my face?"

"No. I'm just...grateful."

Grateful she'd given me a second chance.

Grateful she trusted me enough to let me this close to her.

Grateful, even if I had lost my football career, I'd gotten

something more precious in return.

"Stop that. It makes me feel self-conscious." She leaned forward, her hair hiding her face.

The next time she caught me looking, she bopped me on the tip of the nose with her chopsticks and laughed delightedly at the look of shock on my face. When she fell asleep, I wanted to carry her upstairs, but my knee still wasn't strong enough to hold us both. Instead, I nudged her awake and sent her along to bed. I pushed a kitchen chair under the door handle so it would wake us up if anyone tried to get in.

The blankets were turned down when I got upstairs, and she was wide awake again, staring out of the window into the dark. I pulled the curtains shut, not because I didn't want her seeing out, but because I didn't want anyone else seeing in. I shut off the light and crawled into my side of the bed.

"We need to change the locks."

Her voice was so quiet, so resigned, I could hardly hear her. I could just make out the faint outline of her face. The bed creaked as she rolled over, closer than she'd ever been, and pressed her forehead against mine. I held my hand out and she laced our fingers together.

"It's only a week till Christmas. I know he'll show up at some point, probably on Christmas morning. The more of an impact he makes, the more he ruins things, the happier he'll be."

"Let him show up," I whispered fiercely. "At least if he's here in person, he can't torment you by lurking. He won't do anything illegal because he won't want to tarnish his good-cop image."

"And when he's here, beating on the door, and you can't call the police because they'll take his side? Then what?"

I wished I had my team to back me up. I missed them almost as much as I missed actually playing football. Jackson, Toby, Mitch, Davante, Jakobe. Ray Stalides would think twice before showing up if all of them were here to back us up. But they were an hour away, and they owed me nothing. They were my friends, and always would be, but the team had already moved on. I followed their progress online, and their victory at the state championship was bittersweet. I was still in on the team group text though, so I wasn't entirely out of the loop.

"I'm scared, Felix. And I hate that, because it means he's winning. He thrives on fear. He feeds on it."

"He didn't beat you then, and he won't beat you now."

Her breaths slowly evened out, but I lay awake for a long time, jumping at noises and listening as deeper sleep brought out Hesper's nightmares. I didn't have to ask what they were about—I already knew. When visitation became a matter of crisis, when she wept because she didn't want to see him but had to, I told her to just stop going. So she did. The first night she didn't show for her mandated visit, he came peeling into her driveway, throwing rocks everywhere, stormed up to the door, and slammed his palms against the glass. I had held her while she cowered on the floor, before her temper finally got the best of her fear and she whirled through the front door and confronted him. I had been right on her heels.

It had not gone well.

Afterward, she had been shaking and crying, alternately terrified and furious. It took the police forty minutes to show up; by the time they did, he was long gone, and the damage was done. For weeks afterward she had purple, bruise-like circles under her eyes from nightmare-filled, sleepless nights; every time she saw a vehicle like his, she slid down in the seat to avoid being seen. And when we graduated high school and I could no longer bear to watch her live a life of fear, we had run away across the country together, two best friends seeking a new fresh start away from the place we grew up.

I had foolishly thought it was over, but really, she had never stopped running. Neither of us had. Now her past was about to come knocking on our door, and all I could do was hope we could find a way to end his hold over her once and for all.

IF WE HAD expected Ray to make a move soon, we were mistaken. The semester at Morrow ended. I finalized my spring class schedule and filed a tuition waiver. Hesper worked late with Jasmine decorating for the gala. All quiet on the western front, and when I got a text from Jackson about the team Christmas party, I felt confident we could go without incident.

Well. *We*. Maybe just *I*.

"I don't do parties, and I especially don't do parties with a bunch of muscleheads who introduce themselves to me by saying *damn, girl, you're fine*." Hesper was stretched out on the couch, her legs draped over mine and her sketch pad in her lap.

"*I* was one of those muscleheads. They're my team."

"Your team. Who shrugged you off like an old jacket once you couldn't play anymore," she deadpanned. "Excuse me if I don't have much respect for the way they treated you."

"I'm going to your gala."

"Felix," she said patiently, putting down her pencil. "Don't even try to play the reciprocity card on me. You don't have to go to the gala. If it makes you uncomfortable, I'll go by myself. Because I care about you, and I don't want you to be miserable."

No matter what I said, I'd come out looking like a jackass. I grimaced. "I don't want to leave you here alone while I'm gone."

"I managed just fine for the last three years; I promise you I can last a single night while you go hang out with your dude bro friends." She pulled her legs back, and I missed her warmth immediately. "It's okay if we don't do everything together, you know. I'll stay here and paint."

"You could have Jasmine over for movie night," I suggested.

She narrowed her eyes. "I don't need to be babysat. Go to your dumb party tomorrow, and I'll paint and recharge my introvert batteries. It'll be fine."

"You'll text me if you need anything?"

"Of course. Not that you'll be able to do anything, because you'll be an hour away." She rolled her eyes. "Besides, do you know how hard it's been trying to wrap your present with you hovering all the time?"

"You—you got me a present?"

"Of course I did. It's Christmas. You're my..." She flapped her hand. "My something."

"Boyfriend?"

"Husband. Best friend. Boyfriend. All of the above."

She knew I hadn't grown up with much; my job was only part-time, and we had never exchanged presents. This year though, things were different.

"Calm down. It's nothing fancy, and I don't expect anything in return." She stood up and stretched.

I held my hand out, wiggling my fingers, raising my eyebrows.

Sometimes she was secretive about her drawings. This time, she handed it right over. The corner of the page was filled with my face from the side—she must have drawn me while I was watching TV—but the rest of it contained a dozen or more mask designs, most featuring feathers, others with purple sequins and silvery pearls or covered in a fine mesh of lace. Some had sticks so the mask could be held up; others were threaded with ribbons so they could be tied on.

"You're so talented. Have you thought about making these? Or at least selling the designs?"

"No. But I'm going to make my mask for the gala." She snatched the book back and snapped it shut, smiling. "You'll only get to see which one if you go. And my dress."

Times like this were especially hard for me. I remained perfectly still, trying to recite the digits of pi, or think about how miserable our first preseason football practice was, or remember the agony of the ice water bath I once took on a dare from Jackson. Anything to distract myself from thinking about how she would look in her gala dress and mask—or out of it.

"I have a sincere question, and I don't want you to get offended. I'm genuinely curious."

"Okay. Shoot." She fished between the cushion and the couch arm and came up with a missing pencil, smiling triumphantly.

"I accept everything about you. But since you don't have any...sexual desire." Why was it so easy to have sex, and so hard to talk about it? "Does that mean you're not attracted to me? To anyone?"

It had been a burning question on my mind, and surprisingly, she didn't get angry or embarrassed.

"I don't exactly know how to answer that. It's different for me," she said thoughtfully. She held up a finger, signaling me to wait while she did something on her phone, then passed it to me. She had an image search up, a picture of a sharp silver Corvette filling the screen. "Don't you think that's a gorgeous car?"

"Well, yeah."

"Do you want to sleep with it?"

"What?" I asked, baffled. "No, it's gorgeous to *look* at, how would that even *work—*"

"Exactly. It's called aesthetic attraction. I have *eyes*. I know you're very handsome." She grinned. "You're blushing, and frankly that's adorable. I love your dimples and when I see you, my hands itch to draw you. I find you very aesthetically pleasing, and I don't love you any less for not wanting to have sex with you. It's not *personal*. Do you understand where I'm coming from?"

"I...yeah, I guess I do."

She reached over, put her fingers under my chin, and tipped my head up, her expression suddenly serious and her eyes vulnerable.

"I need to know. Is that a deal breaker? Someday, will it

make you mad that I can't give you what you want? Will you go and find someone else who can?"

"No," I said flatly. "I'm not sure about a lot of things, but I'm sure about that."

"Okay." She hesitated. "Thank you for being honest with me."

Hesper leaned forward, and I sat very still as she brushed her lips across mine. Every cell in my body lit up, but I didn't move, and she smiled tentatively.

"That was less terrifying than I anticipated. Now, go call Jackson and tell him you'll be baching it at the Christmas party." She stood up. "I have a mask to make. Shoo."

I drove Calamity the next day, and I didn't expect how raw and fresh the bitterness would be when I returned to campus—to my old dorm, no less. Jackson was absolutely delighted, hugging me and offering me a can of beer, which I promptly refused. I couldn't even handle the smell of liquor too close. Maybe it was because my mom was an alcoholic, and I didn't want to end up like her, or maybe I just couldn't stomach the stuff; either way, it made me the designated driver of the group. He shrugged, like it was my loss, and chugged the can, crushing it when he was done in his powerful fist.

"The old ball and chain let you out of the house for one last hurrah with your boys?"

"Don't call her that." I sat down on the couch, looking around; surprisingly, very little had changed. Jackson had a new roommate, another football player who was apparently already at the party, which wasn't set to start for another half hour.

His smile fell. "I'm sorry, man. I forget sometimes you

take stuff so serious. I didn't mean anything by it."

"No worries. I know you didn't, I'm just...nervous."

It was the truth. These guys had once been more or less my brothers; maybe Hesper was onto something. Maybe how they'd treated me *wasn't* okay—like I didn't even exist anymore. But they had invited me to the party, which meant they still considered me part of the team. That had to count for something. Maybe they didn't know what to say; everyone knew how much I'd lost that day on the field. An NFL scout had been there. I could have had *everything*.

But the things I'd ended up with instead weren't so bad.

"Spit it out, dude. You got something on your mind. I can tell." Jackson tapped his forehead.

"Can I borrow a suit?" I blurted.

Ah, the crux of the problem. I had agreed to go to the gala with Hesper without a single article of black-tie clothing to my name, just my dad's old blazer and a too-small button-up. I hated it, hated only being able to pitch in on groceries and gas and never having enough to take Hesper out on a nice date or even enough to rent a suit for a night. Jackson stood back and sized me up.

"Yeah, I bet I have one that would fit you."

He was on scholarship, but he didn't *need* to be. His parents could easily have paid for his college. They were together, earning six-digit salaries. I'd gone with him a few times to visit them over spring break. I had never been jealous, because I thought if I worked hard I could make all my dreams come true without being born into it.

I could still be a coach. I could still find something I was as passionate about as I had been about playing football.

Jackson dug in his closet. He tossed several suits out on

the bed, and I picked up a black one. I pulled the jacket on over my T-shirt. It was a little snug in the arms, but close enough nobody would notice it wasn't mine.

"Thanks. I owe you one."

"Nah, don't sweat it. I haven't had to wear these since I changed majors. Keep it as long as you need. What's it for? Big job interview?"

"No, a work thing. With Hesper."

"Tell me, Felix. Is she for real? Because this sounds like more than playing pretend for free college."

Damnit, I forgot—for all that he was annoying and clueless most of the time—he was pretty perceptive when it came to the things that mattered.

"Yes. It's...very real."

"Good for you, dude." He clapped me on the shoulder. "Good luck with her. Maybe someday you'll renew your vows? I can be your best man next time."

I smiled. "Count on it."

I stashed the suit, dress shirt, and tie carefully in Calamity's hatch before I loaded up Jackson and drove across campus to Mitch's house. Music pulsed so loud I could hear it outside, and I already had a headache, but deep down, I was too desperate to still be a part of this—to hold on, at least for a little bit longer, to who I was and the friends I had before the accident.

As it turned out, the music—despite its volume—was just a bunch of rock and roll renditions of classic Christmas songs, and everyone sat piled on the living room floor around an Xbox, drinking eggnog (which I assumed was spiked, given how merrily and off-key they were singing along) and playing on their phones.

"Felix!" Davante cheered from his spot on the floor, and Mitch stuck his head out of the kitchen door and waved a plate of crackers.

"Snacks in the kitchen! Help yourself."

"Congrats on the season." I smiled, surprised to find most of the bitterness had melted away. I was genuinely happy for them.

All the same, the mood in the room shifted, and nobody would meet my eyes.

Most of them moseyed off to play festive pong—which was really just beer pong using red and green ping-pong balls in plastic cups with snowflakes printed on the sides. I settled in on the couch next to Jackson, and Mitch came in with a tray full of candies.

"Rum balls?" He waggled his eyebrows. "My grandma's famous recipe."

He plopped down on the floor and regaled me with play-by-play details of all the games I had missed, including my replacement's glorious fourth-quarter catch of Davante's Hail Mary, winning us the game and the championship. Toby handed me a controller, taking advantage of the raucous pong game going on in the dining room, before freezing.

"Felix Morlan, you got *married*?"

Wearing my ring had become second nature—I had forgotten I had it on. It was like an extension of my skin. But of course they would notice. I snatched the controller away, but now both Toby and Mitch were leaning in, gawking at the golden band on my finger.

"You weren't even dating anyone when you left!"

"You move *quick,* dude. Who's the poor sucker who

married you?"

"My high school sweetheart." I flushed; I wasn't sure why. Hesper didn't embarrass me, and it wasn't actually a lie.

"Why didn't you bring her along? She could have hung out with Alison and Mina." Mitch gestured to the deck, where Davante's and Jakobe's girlfriends sat perched on the rail, their heads bent together over a phone.

"She's not big on parties."

"You'd have told us about this girl if you were dating her. What happened—did you knock her up?"

Before, I would have wrestled with him, got him in a headlock, and rubbed my knuckles into the top of his head until he apologized, laughing. Now it was so much worse, because of what it implied about Hesper—about the nature of our relationship. Like she was just some girl I went to school with and slept with on a whim, like we had some mandatory shotgun wedding.

I punched Toby, my fingers curled in as my knuckles connected with his face. He shouted and swung back but I was on him, diving off the couch and straddling him, hitting him again. He got a punch in on me and blood gushed from my lip, and I was still swinging when Jackson got hold of me and dragged me off him. I struggled, the adrenaline of the fight buzzing and the rage making me desperate to hit Toby again.

"What the hell's wrong with you?" Toby shouted, scrambling up off the floor and away from me while Mitch sprinted for the kitchen.

"Don't bleed on my carpet!" he bellowed over his shoulder.

"Don't go running your mouth when you don't know anything about her!" I yelled, squirming against Jackson's grasp, my knee screaming in agony over my abrupt dive to the floor.

"Felix. Felix!" Jackson shouted in my ear, and I finally went limp, all the fight in me gone in a flash of horror. I had *punched* a former teammate. "Chill, man! He didn't mean anything by it!"

I grabbed Hesper's keys and headed for the door, half mortified, half filled with a vicious sort of satisfaction.

"That was out of line, Tobes," Jackson snapped.

"It was just a joke!"

"Yeah? Well, it wasn't funny."

I slipped outside, the cold night air stinging my burning cheeks, and Jackson followed on my heels—because even though he was a tool sometimes, he was a good guy at heart. A good friend.

"This party is dumb. Let's get out of here."

"You don't have to leave. I'll wait in the Jeep till you're ready to go—and please apologize to Mitch." I yanked my shirt up and held the hem against my mouth to staunch the bleeding, then added scathingly, "But don't apologize to Toby, because he's a jackass."

He smiled. "So are you."

"Yeah. I know."

"Take me home and go back to your girl. Wouldn't you rather spend Christmas Eve with her instead of a bunch of knuckleheads anyway?"

Of course I would. I wished I would have realized it sooner. They had changed, and so had I—too much, maybe, to pretend we had enough in common to hang out.

"Thank you, Jackson. You're a good friend."

I dropped him back off; I had spent longer driving to Pearcy than I had at the actual party. Calamity was slow to start, and the engine sputtered, but she finally kicked down. Someday she was going to leave either Hesper or me sitting on the side of the road, but at least she had the good taste not to do it the night before Christmas.

9:13 PM

Why does Santa Claus go down the chimney on Christmas Eve?

9:14 PM

Because it SOOTS him!

9:17 PM

Does this mean you're headed home early?

9:17 PM

On my way.

I started the long drive home—to Hesper's house, the place I belonged.

CHAPTER NINE

HESPER

I WASN'T AN I-told-you-so kind of girl, especially when Felix slipped inside—with a split lip, no less. I raised my eyebrows but didn't ask. He carried a suit on a hanger, looking sheepish.

"Jackson's suit. Sorry it won't match your dress."

"How could it? I haven't even shown you my dress."

"Touché."

He hung it up in the living room closet, where he still kept his clothes despite the rather alarming fact that we basically shared a bedroom now—and he was as good as his word. He didn't put a single toe over the line, and I felt certain if I told him he was making me uncomfortable, he'd back right off.

Because I finally believed he wanted this to work as badly as I did.

Felix had walked through the door between the living room and the kitchen no less than six times before he caught sight of what I had hung from the facing. He cut his eyes around at me nervously, and my lungs tightened with affection, because his expression clearly said, *are you sure*?

Mistletoe—a big bunch of it in a heart-shape, dangling from a hook.

He made sure not to linger under it too long, zipping into the kitchen and coming back with the last few snickerdoodles, warmed in the microwave, and milk for both of us. We sat on the couch and turned on old black-and-white movies, polishing off the cookies and admiring the Christmas tree and lights. It was cozy inside, and snow was falling outside; if I'd ever had such a nice Christmas Eve, I certainly couldn't recall it.

Something was bothering him, but I gave him time—because he didn't pry, and I wanted to return the favor. Jimmy Stewart had realized his own importance and Clarence the angel had gotten his wings before he finally spoke.

"I punched someone."

"I gathered." I leaned forward, tracing my fingertip along his lip.

"Do you ever get anyone at work making horrible comments about...us? About this?" He gestured vaguely.

"People think it's strange. They know I was very single and very uninterested, and it takes them by surprise. Why? Do you care what people say?"

He thought about it for a long time. "No. Not really. I just...don't want them to hurt you."

"I appreciate that, but I'm pretty tough. It's not the outer demons I struggle with. I'll fight anyone—the only voice I can't ignore is my own."

He checked his watch. "Merry Christmas, Hesper."

Not H, not Hes. Hesper.

"Merry Christmas, Felix." I stood up and unplugged the lights strung around the tree.

Before he could head up the stairs, I grabbed the corner of his shirt—grimacing when I saw the blood on the hem— and pulled him under the mistletoe. He stood still, letting me lead and go at my own pace, and I loved him for it, appreciated it more than he would ever know. I held my arms out and he moved in for a hug, and we stood that way for a while. I was still adapting to the feel of being in someone's arms, still trying to figure out if I had any sensual attraction. I liked holding hands. I liked sitting together on the couch. I was starting to like hugs—but only from Felix. My comfort levels were changing every day.

"Is this okay?" he murmured.

"Would you accept me if I didn't think it was okay?"

"Of course."

"I'll keep you posted." I cocked my head. "I think I like being held."

I curled one hand around the back of his neck and rested the other one on his cheek. He leaned down obligingly, and I ran my thumb along his cheekbone, marveling at all the things that had always made him so captivating and fun to draw. I moved the hand on his neck up, reveling in the softness of his hair—longer now than it had been since high school.

"I'm so jealous of your eyelashes," I whispered.

His only response was a strangled-sounding "Hmmm," and I realized he was taut as a bowstring. Standing this still was taking a concentrated effort on his part.

"Thank you for your patience." I stood on my tiptoes and pressed my lips to his.

It was less scary this time, but also did absolutely nothing for me. No fireworks went off; my skin didn't feel electric. His hands twitched where they were settled on my waist, and his lips parted slightly, and I pulled away, thoroughly disgusted because *wet* and *germy* and I knew inevitably I was bound to encounter his tongue or his teeth and the thought made me want to positively gag.

"I'm sorry," he said quickly, and I realized I had backpedaled several steps, only stopping when I bumped into the kitchen table.

"Don't be." I resisted the urge to spit in the trash can. How many romance novels talked about how people *tasted*? I didn't want to *taste* Felix. My stomach heaved. "It's me, it's all me, I'm just, I'm dysfunctional—"

"It's okay if you don't like kissing me."

"It's not *you*," I moaned, frustrated. "It's the idea of kissing. I wouldn't put my mouth on anyone, and I don't want anyone putting their mouth on me!"

"Hey. Calm down. We don't have to."

"Who wants a girlfriend they can't kiss?" I turned and tried to storm upstairs, but he caught my hand—gentle, not insistent, so I didn't pull away.

"I want you any way I can have you. And this—this is enough for me. Of course I want to kiss you, and of course I want to sleep with you." Hearing him say it out loud made my skin crawl, made my stomach tense with fear. "But I also want what's best for you, and if those things aren't, well, I'll learn to live with that. Because I'd rather have you in this capacity than not have you at all."

"You say that now," I sighed, and I retreated up the stairs.

I lay in the dark and listened to the sounds of him moving around downstairs, the sink running briefly while he brushed his teeth, the uneven thump of his bare feet on the stairs, his routine as familiar to me as my own. I had grown so used to this. I wasn't sure how I'd cope with the silence once he got fed up and tired of how very little I had to offer him.

"No crying on Christmas," he said from the doorway, silhouetted by the hall light behind him.

He had no way of knowing. I was a quiet crier, and it was too dark to see me. But he could tell anyway, because he had been the other half of my heart for as long as I could remember. He knew me almost as well as I knew myself. When he sank down on the bed, pulling the covers up, I reached over, bridging the gap between us, and pulled him closer to me, an awkward tangle of arms and legs.

"I like this," I confessed. It was easier to talk in the dark. "I'm sorry that it's all I can do."

"Don't ever apologize for being who you are, Hesper."

"You'll be giving up a lot."

"You're worth it." He bumped his forehead against mine gently.

IN THE MORNING I woke up first, freezing in horror because we were entirely too close—I could feel every inch of him pressed against me, separated only by our thin, well-worn pajamas. It wasn't his fault; it was an involuntary reaction by his body, and it was awkward but inevitable. I extracted myself as carefully as possible, relieved to get a bit of distance, and padded down the stairs quietly. I slipped into my painting room and pulled out the one I had done for him—wrapped now, but I knew it by heart. Oil laid on in thick smears, drying in beautiful ridges, depicting the depth of the night broken up by concentric rings of warm light. The snow in the distance was smooth, shaded with subtle color-tinged grays, with more impasto giving texture to the drifts in the foreground. And of course I had painted *us*, subtle silhouettes, focusing so intently on that moment of tension between us while both of us had waited for the other to break and finally make a move.

I leaned it against the Christmas tree, then went to the kitchen to make breakfast. I threw some frozen cinnamon French toast sticks on a baking sheet and slid it into the oven. I'd popped some syrup into the microwave to heat up when I heard Felix's slow, shuffling steps down the stairs. His eyes were enormous when he came into the kitchen carrying the painting, his hair mussed from sleep.

"You're...giving me this?"

"That is the idea of a Christmas present, yes."

"Smarty-pants." He smiled anyway, his most radiant and genuine one, the one I loved best. The one I could almost—but never exactly—capture. "It's stunning. I wish you'd consider doing a show."

"Never. I would make myself sick dreading it, fail to

muster the nerve to attend the reception, and if I got negative reviews, I'd hate myself so much I'd never paint again. And I *need* to paint—I need it like I need to breathe."

"I get that. Thank you—I love it. Will it make you anxious if I hang it?"

"Maybe a little."

"We live in *the same house*," he laughed. "We share a bedroom! Why would you give it to me if I have to hide it from you? It's impossible for me to enjoy it anywhere you won't see it."

"That's fair. I guess you can hang it—on *your* side of the room." I put on oven mitts and grabbed breakfast out of the oven. We sat down at the table and ate right off the pan.

"I sort of got you something too. It's, uh...not much. I promise next year will be better. I'll be about to graduate then, and my knee will be healed up, I hope, so I can get a better job." Embarrassed, he handed me a stack of tickets printed on card stock.

Honestly, I was too emotional over the idea that he still planned to be around next Christmas to try to tease him out of his self-consciousness. The tickets all said something different. Breakfast in bed. A date at a museum. A movie of my choice, even if he hated it. Several "shut up" tickets, promising he would leave me alone to let me paint or recharge my introvert batteries. (I noted, with a smile, that these said REUSABLE! all around the border.)

"They're perfect. Thank you."

I leaned over and kissed his cheek, because for some reason, that didn't set off all the alarm bells and ratchet my anxiety up to a nonfunctional level. It seemed to be okay, so long as I was the one initiating and there was no physical reaction on his part. His jaw was stubbly where he hadn't shaved yet. It was oddly endearing, and we sat at the table, eating our French toast sticks and holding hands while he rattled off every Christmas joke he knew and I rolled my eyes, trying not to laugh because it seemed like a bad idea to encourage him.

For the first Christmas in years, I wasn't alone.

JASMINE CAME OVER on New Year's Eve, because she said—in not so many words—she didn't trust me to actually get dressed and show up. She wasn't exactly wrong. For all the excitement of the dress and delicate, handcrafted mask I'd painstakingly created, the anxiety that always accompanied social events had been gaining momentum every day since Christmas. If she hadn't shown up with a makeup kit and a bag of hair styling tools, I probably would have spent the night in my sweatpants, eating pizza and playing board games with Felix, consequences with the college be damned.

"Out! Shoo! You can't see her till she's ready," she said bossily, pushing him out despite his startled, vaguely worried expression and shutting the door in his face.

I liked Jasmine very much, but she was...a lot. I was nothing but a tangled mess of boundaries—*dozens* of boundaries that crisscrossed and got jumbled up and never let anyone near me. Jasmine had no boundaries at all, and she was delightful but utterly exhausting. She whirled across the room, threw open my closet, and tossed a button-up blouse over her shoulder and onto the bed.

"Put that on, so you won't mess up your hair and

makeup when you change." She kept her back turned, and when I'd swapped out my old ratty T-shirt for the blouse, she whisked me into the chair in front of the vanity.

"I don't even know how to put on makeup, why do I have to wear *makeup*?"

She looked appalled. "Are you telling me you didn't even wear makeup to your wedding?"

"Of course I didn't. We didn't even take any pictures—what's the point?"

"Stop being so practical, Hesper, it is *exhausting*."

She spread my dress out on my lap and dropped more than a dozen tiny, round black containers filled with eyeshadow on top of it. She weeded out colors one by one until only three or four were left. I closed my eyes and tried not to flinch as she expertly faded two colors together, then applied something wet.

"Liquid eyeliner. You need wings," she said, as if that explained anything at all to someone who could count on one hand all the times in their life they'd worn makeup.

"Butterflies have wings. Birds have wings. Why do you think my eyes need wings? My eyes are fine."

"Your eyes are lovely," she agreed. "But you've spent how many years hiding at Morrow? You're gonna shine tonight. Don't get me wrong, you'd shine without the makeup, without the updo. But I want you to feel confident. I want you to feel as gorgeous as you are. You said you didn't feel like a princess at prom. You deserve that tonight."

She handed me a tube of liquid lipstick, still wrapped in plastic. "I know you're kind of particular about germs, so I got you one to keep. This stuff means business. It won't come off no matter how much you kiss at midnight." She gave me a wink and I wanted to crawl under my chair. Maybe someday I'd find the courage to be honest and explain to her how I really was—how suggestive comments would never apply to me.

"You're too good at this," I marveled as she expertly turned my wild waves into hundreds of tiny ringlets, leaving most of them loose around my shoulders and braiding the excess on the sides, then pinning it into a halo around my head like a crown.

"Thank you! If I hadn't gone into teaching, I'd have done cosmetology. I love this stuff." She sprawled across my bed, closing her eyes. "Put on the dress."

I complied, and she screamed when I told her to open her eyes, startling me. She bounced up and down on the balls of her feet.

"You're stunning! Everyone at Morrow's gonna wish they were Felix tonight. Where are your shoes?"

I pointed wordlessly to a pair of glittery iridescent canvas sneakers that sat neatly under the edge of the bed.

"If you can rock the dress and the makeup like a fairy princess, I guess I can let the shoes slide." Jasmine smiled.

As soon as I put them on, I felt a little more myself—the one piece of Hesper amid the dreamy handkerchief dress and dramatic eye makeup that made me look like I was on my way to a fae revel instead of a college scholarship gala. I sat on the edge of the bed, knocking the rubber tips of my shoes together where they dangled a few inches from the floor while Jasmine got ready. I barely had time to close my eyes before she unzipped the dress she'd come in and shook her gala dress out of the garment bag she'd brought with her. It was the orange of a dying fire, slim and smooth until it got to her knees, where it belled out into ruffles.

"See—isn't it more fun getting ready together?"

"I have to admit," I agreed grudgingly, leaning forward and watching her do her own form of art.

Instead of wearing a mask, Jasmine was applying thick liquid makeup with wedge-shaped sponges, painting her own. She rimmed her eyes with yellow, fading to orange and edged in red tongues of flame. Using tweezers and tiny rhinestones from a little plastic packet she kept in her kit, she applied jewels like beautiful sparks. She coiled her hair into a messy bun and put a red-and-gold feathered band around it. This wasn't a costume party, it was a proper gala, but I had to give her props—she had made herself into a phoenix.

"You're an artist. How did I not realize this?"

"I like makeup, and I like fashion." She shrugged, adding dangling earrings—a cascade of red and orange sequins—to her ensemble.

"That *is* art, Jasmine. That counts."

She looked embarrassed but pleased. "Thanks, Hesper. Did you get a mask?"

"Not exactly. I made one." I opened the vanity drawer I'd stashed it in and handed it over.

"Oh my God!" She handled it like it was made of spun glass.

The top edge was lined with lace, the closest I could find to match the hem of my dress, and the rest of it was covered in small sequins in as many shades of purple as I could find, layered and overlapping slightly with no identical colors touching. The bottom was trimmed with a line of tiny, iridescent plastic pearls. I had punched holes in the sides for the lilac ribbon used to tie it.

"You probably don't want to put that on till we're ready to go, but I can't wait to see the whole ensemble."

Jasmine spun me around, expertly laced up my dress, and knotted the bow securely at the small of my back. It didn't even feel awkward; either my medicine was balancing out my adverse reactions or I had actually become comfortable enough with her that human contact no longer felt like the end of the world. She held out her arm. I linked mine with it, and she threw open the door dramatically. She was graceful on sparkly gold stilettos, easily five or six inches taller than me, but I felt solid and comfortable in my sneakers. Felix was waiting at the table, "reading the newspaper"—which meant, of course, that the newspaper was spread out on the table and his phone was sitting on top of it, a puzzle game open on the screen. He looked bored, sitting there in a borrowed suit with his hair sticking up slightly in the back.

"I present to you—Hesper Stalides-Morlan." Jasmine bowed with a flourish. I didn't correct her.

The look he gave me would have vaporized standing water, but instead of glancing away I met his gaze evenly. He didn't crack a joke to ease the tension. I didn't want him to. *This is why I didn't enjoy prom,* I realized. *This is what was missing.* We had gone together as best friends. This...this was something entirely different, the do-over I never realized I wanted. He looked at me like I was the only thing in the world.

"You two need a minute?" Jasmine raised an eyebrow. "Or a room, maybe?"

The spell was broken. Felix grinned, sticking his foot

out from under the table to reveal sneakers just like mine, but black instead of sparkly.

"Informal shoe twins!" He walked up to me and bumped the rubber toes of our shoes together.

He smelled like peppermint toothpaste and aftershave. I could count every one of his eyelashes this close. As always, my hands curled slightly, desperate for a pencil and a pad of paper. He was beautiful, and he didn't even know it, and I loved him all the more for it. My chest hurt with it; my heart had never felt so full.

It didn't feel like we were pretending to be in a relationship anymore. It felt *real*.

The doorbell rang; a harried-looking delivery driver was holding a thermal bag, their shirt proclaiming "Pizza New Year!" instead of "It's a New Year," and I groaned while the other two chuckled. Felix reached over me to pay, his arm brushing my bare shoulder. The three of us sat at the kitchen table, devouring pizza in our formalwear, like a strange but enjoyable echo of the parties we'd had growing up.

"Well, I hate to eat and run, but I want to get there early and make sure everything is in order. Call it my type A personality." Jasmine winked. "Now that you're dressed, can I trust you to show?"

"Yes, Jasmine." I smiled, feeling an odd pang.

Would she still be my friend after the gala was over—when there was no mutual obligation to tie us together? We had very little in common, really, other than working at Morrow. But she blew us a kiss and gave us a little wave on her way out the door, and it gave me hope.

"That girl is exhausting," Felix huffed, flopping backward into his chair.

I sat down, too, and doodled—a slice of pizza with cheese oozing over the sides, banana pepper rings peeking out from under discs of pepperoni; a mask for Jasmine, crisscrossed with diamond shapes and a rhinestone where each of them intersected, feathers bursting in a triumphant arc over the top. I felt Felix's eyes on my hands, watching me work, though he didn't interrupt.

"This is our first date." His voice was surprisingly nervous, wavering.

"It's no different than anything else. We get to skip all those awkward first-date quirks. Besides, how is a date scary when you already married me?"

"Because when I did, it wasn't real. Now it is. Now I stand to lose a lot more."

"Don't. And if you're uncomfortable, if you just want to stay home and play board games and cards and watch TV, I'm fine with that too. Jasmine will get over it." It was unusual, being the reassuring one. I was almost always an anxious mess—but this, us, I was finally sure about.

Was it really a first date when you knew each other's sleeping positions and had spent your whole lives taking care of each other? All other dates made me nervous, but this left me with nothing but anticipation. He held his hand out, and I placed mine in it. We locked the door behind us as we headed for Calamity.

How did Jasmine drive in those heels? I was grateful for my good old tennis shoes as we crossed campus, parked, and headed inside—where, in the week interim, I'd managed to forget the committee had made the gala kind of magical. The box bushes outside were covered in a net of twinkle lights, and we slipped through the big, glass double doors. Another committee member, a girl whose name I couldn't remember who worked in the financial aid department, sat at a table with an elegant navy throw over it, a clipboard and a cash box at the ready.

"Is this your date?" She raised an eyebrow at Felix, which only went higher when she spotted our rings. "Husband?"

"Yes," he cut in, reaching across the table to give her a firm handshake, his other hand still holding mine.

"Nice to meet you, Hesper's Man," she laughed. "Go on in; committee members and their plus-ones are free."

We stood in the doorway, on the threshold of something both daunting and thrilling.

"Need some help tying on your mask?" Felix held out his hand tentatively.

I pressed it to my face and turned away. He reached around and grabbed the ribbons, then tied them together beneath the twisted crown of curls Jasmine had put in my hair. He leaned down, his lips close to my ear, his breath on my shoulders sending goose bumps up my arms.

"It's perfect. You ready?"

I threaded my fingers back through his as we headed toward the sounds from the gala drifting from the open doors at the end of the hall. I had to admit, decorating the conference room had been more fun than I had anticipated, and the payoff was amazing. The overhead fluorescents had been dimmed, the string lights on the tables glowing gently and the lush, feathered arrangements glinting in the half-light. A rainbow of people in dresses and suits with button-up shirts that matched them milled around, making friendly small talk and carrying flutes of sparkling champagne.

I found our table and saw—with no surprise—that Jasmine had seated herself on one side of me and Felix on the other. One of her many, many lists was lying neatly at her spot with an ink pen, most of the items checked off, but she was nowhere to be found. I craned my neck, searching, and found her a few tables away, a spot of orange like a flame in the darkness. She was seated next to a girl in a turquoise dress, and they leaned together conspiratorially, their hands touching slightly, their pinkie fingers hooked together.

"Her ex," I murmured. "Well, maybe not anymore."

"Good for her." He snagged two glasses from a passing waiter and handed one to me—water, since neither of us drank.

Morrow's band were gathered on a set of risers in the corner of the room, providing soft instrumental music. Most people were chatting, but a few couples were dancing, and this seemed to be what Felix was waiting for. He stood up, holding out his hand. I could make out the bulge of his knee brace under the pants of his suit, but his limp was mostly gone and he hadn't used his crutches in almost a week.

"Don't overdo it."

"I won't." He smiled, sweeping me up into his arms.

People around us muttered disapprovingly about our shoes, my unconventional dress and over-the-top mask, the fact that Felix's shoulders were obviously wider than Jackson's, pulling the jacket tight across his back. None of that mattered.

"Why didn't I ask you to dance in high school?" he whispered, one arm curled around my waist, our entwined hands at the level of our shoulders.

"Maybe because I spent our senior prom having a panic attack?" I suggested. "Besides, I don't think I was ready then. I think we were supposed to wait until both of us could handle it."

"Why aren't you freaking out now? You hate social situations."

"It doesn't feel social." I paused as he spun me, my skirt swirling out around me and falling back against my legs. "It feels like it's just us. Besides, I got help. Amazing how, when your brain doesn't manage its own serotonin right, all it takes sometimes is a chemical reset."

"I'm proud of you for getting help. It makes me happy to see you happy."

"It took a lot of courage," I confessed in a whisper. We had mostly stopped dancing; I had laid my head on his chest, listening to his steady heartbeat as we swayed back and forth. "I thought I wouldn't be me if I got help—that I would lose who I was. Turns out I'm even *more* me without the constant klaxon of panic and hopelessness drowning me out. I'm a much better version of myself now—though there's always plenty of room for improvement."

"I love every version of you there has ever been, even when I was too young to realize it. I wasted time."

"I spent a lot of jealous years thinking I could never have this. That it wasn't fair to ask it of anyone, for this kind of commitment without anything in return."

"You can't believe that, Hesper. It's not a table or chart of transactions. Even if it wasn't me...and I hope it is, I hope it's *always* me." He closed his eyes. "You deserve as much affection as you want, without being expected to reciprocate in a way that makes you uncomfortable."

"Wow. I'm not the only one who's come a long way." Tears—happy ones—collected in the inside lip of my mask and trickled down the sides of my face.

"What do you mean?" He didn't sound angry, just confused.

"When I came out, I was...scared. Upset. And when you acted like I was just being sensitive, like I would just get over it." I swallowed. "It hurt. I thought this wouldn't, couldn't, work. But you've spent every day since then proving it can if we both want it bad enough."

"Oh, great, now *I'm* crying," he sniffed, dropping my hand to rub his arm across his face.

I laughed, wondering if maybe someday I'd get used to the idea of kissing him. I might, or I might not, but either way was fine. We were still Hesper and Felix, us against the world, and if we wanted it to work it would. Nothing we could or couldn't do would mean we were broken—or if we were, we were lucky. His jagged edges lined up with mine.

The band slowed and a woman stood at a well-lit podium to give the keynote speech before dinner was served. Jasmine was obviously not returning to her seat—I watched her slip out of the door, hand in hand with the girl in the blue dress. I settled in next to Felix, digging in my clutch for my cell and a tissue. I was sure my eye makeup was running down my face, though my actual tears had dried.

"The speech will be boring. I'd much rather be dancing."

I patted Felix's knee absently. "It won't be so bad. We can dance again after dinner."

"Can I text you puns under the table?"

"Behave!" I swatted his arm.

"This is my very best behavior, I assure you."

"Behave better, then. I'm going to step out for a second before the speech starts. Watch my stuff."

I felt his eyes on my back all the way to the door. The girl managing the guest list was gone now that the gala was underway, leaving me alone in the empty hallway. While the party didn't send me straight into an anxiety attack like it would have a few years ago, it was still nicer out here. It was cool, quiet, and I walked briskly to the bathroom.

I washed my hands, then washed my face, sorry that Jasmine's beautiful makeup work was gone but unable to tolerate the raccoon eyes I had going after my little crying jag while we danced. I still couldn't believe we had made it here—that so little had changed, and yet so much.

I headed back down the hall when I heard a long, low whistle from the vestibule doors.

I didn't even have to turn around to know who it was. I broke into a run, grateful for my sneakers, making a dash for the gala. I let out my loudest scream, surely there were security guards close—

A hand curled around my arm, hard enough to bruise.

"Don't cause a scene. This silly rebellion is over. It's time to come home."

Shit.

Shit.

My father.

CHAPTER TEN

FELIX

MY HEAD WAS still buzzing from my dance with Hesper, drowning out the lady who was giving the keynote address—and that was fine. I didn't want to waste a single solitary brain cell on anything else. My dad had said to prove myself to her, and it looked like I'd finally done it. I'd learned so much about her, about myself, about *us* and the way we existed in each other's orbits. About how those orbits were changing all the time, shrinking and pulling us closer together.

I waited. And I waited.

Maybe she's hyperventilating. Maybe she's having a

panic or anxiety attack. Maybe things came crashing down on her and she can't function. The longer I sat, the more worried I got. Her keys were in her bag; her cell was on the table. There was no way she would walk home in the cold on New Year's Eve, and no way she would leave without telling me. Not after the scare when I had broken into her painting room. She had promised.

I snatched her phone, all at once surprised and exasperated that she was still using her high school student ID as a PIN, and pulled up a message to Jasmine.

7:36 PM

This is Felix and maybe an emergency. Are you still on campus? Have you seen Hesper?

Surely if anyone knew where she might have gone it would be Jasmine. I had never seen anyone take to Hesper's eccentricities quite like her—and never seen Hesper accept anyone into her circle quite so easily. Maybe this was a girl thing. I gathered her clutch and mask and slipped out into the hall.

It was empty. I lurked outside the bathroom for a minute, hesitating, but her safety was more important than my dignity. I charged inside. Every stall door was open and empty. Real fear started to clutch at my stomach, and I hurried for the vestibule doors, and there, caught in one of them, was a tattered, sheer purple scarf—like the skirt of her dress.

Hesper's phone rang.

"Felix? Did you find her?" Jasmine asked breathlessly.

"No."

"Check by her Jeep. I'll call security."

I gave her my own number so she could call me back. Even from the door I could see Calamity was parked right where we'd left her; still, I favored my bad leg but managed a shuffling sort of run. My phone's flashlight app illuminated the vehicle, but I rattled the door handle and it was still locked. The driver's seat was still pushed forward to accommodate her shorter frame. There was an empty spot a few cars down that hadn't been there when we parked, and I walked it carefully, shining my phone's light on the ground, searching for another piece of fabric or something, anything, to tell me she'd been here.

I turned to head for the building when I saw the purple, glittery bobby pins scattered on the pavement. They matched her dress. Jasmine had done her hair. They *had* to be hers.

My phone rang, a shrill sound in the cold, quiet night, and I answered before the first full ring was up.

"I have the guest list. Come look it over with me and see if you recognize anyone. Security is pulling the camera footage."

I scrolled through Hesper's missed calls, a chill seizing me.

I hoped I was wrong.

I wasn't.

"Is there another Stalides on the list?"

"What, like, family?" She sounded relieved. "You think she might have left with family?"

"Not willingly. Ray Stalides?"

She went through the list of attendees, whispering their names to herself. "Yeah, I see him. He contributed a pretty hefty sum—a gold level donor."

At the end of the day, Hesper was right. An order of protection wouldn't have meant a thing in the world to him, because he had always treated everyone and everything like his personal possessions. Did it surprise me, really, that he had bought his way in here, simply taken her because her will, the law, none of it really mattered to him?

No.

Of course it didn't.

She had been so afraid she had thrown up at the sound of his voice on the message machine. I had *promised* her I would watch out for her, and now she was God knows where, probably scared half out of her mind, while he berated her and abused her and convinced her she was the one in the wrong. It was what he had always done, would always do given a chance.

Why hadn't she taken her phone?

"*Felix*!" Jasmine screamed; I wasn't sure how long she'd been talking while my panic spiraled out of control. "Do I need to call the police?"

"Yes," I choked out.

"Okay. I'm going to hang up now. Meet me at the security office."

She hung up, and for once I was grateful for her bossiness because I needed some direction, someone to tell me what to do because I knew her dad was a trash bag but *this*—this—I made myself take deep, even breaths. I was equipped to handle Hesper's meltdowns, but this was the first time I'd experienced one myself. I couldn't afford to freak out now. Not when she was relying on me. Because I knew where they were going, where he would have taken her: home to Missouri, which meant he had a long drive ahead of him.

If we drove fast enough, we might be able to catch up. He only had a twenty-minute head start.

I wanted to hop in Calamity and start driving, but when I thought with my brain instead of with my panic, I knew the smart thing to do was go with someone else. We could drive through the night that way, and if we did catch up, I'd need backup. Between my bad knee and my compromised judgment—my fear for Hesper ruled my every impulse—it would not go well. My hands were shaking when I dialed Jackson's number.

It rang five times before he answered, thumping bass and a cacophony of voices almost drowning him out. He had to shout to be heard.

"What's up?"

"I need your help." I strode down the hall toward the security office. My phone beeped with call-waiting—Jasmine. "Please."

"Hold on, bro." The noise level dropped significantly. "You okay?"

I shouldered my way through the door. Jasmine had changed into jeans and a pink hooded sweatshirt, a duffel bag with her orange dress peeking out on her lap. She shared a seat with a cute blonde girl, leaning over a security guard's shoulder. The image frozen on the screen confirmed my worst fear—Hesper, struggling against a balding man in a suit, her mouth twisted in a scream. He was older, grayer, but I still recognized Hesper's father. On his hip was the thing that would make it almost impossible to stop him.

A badge.

"Felix. You there?" Jackson asked, his tone uneasy.

"Are you sober?"

"Yeah—what's the point of getting drunk *before* midnight? Why?"

"How fast can you get to Morrow? Hesper's in trouble. I need backup."

"Stay put. I'll be there soon."

He hung up on me but that was fine—it simply meant he was on his way, because he always came through in the clutch. Jasmine put down her cellphone, pale under her amazing painted mask. Her lipstick was smudged and her eyes were wide and frightened.

It had only been a few hours ago that she had kicked me out of Hesper's bedroom—*our* bedroom—to do their makeup.

"The police are on their way. I called in an abduction. It's her dad, so he won't hurt her, right?"

"I wish I could tell you he wouldn't, but..." I scrubbed my hands over my face. "I know where he's taking her, and if he gets her there, back on his home turf...it's not gonna be pretty. My friend Jackson Maddox is on his way here, and we're going after them."

"I'm coming too."

"No."

"What do you mean, *no*?" She put her hands on her hips, glaring.

"I mean Ray has no respect for women, and it'll be a miracle if we get Hesper back unharmed. I'm not dragging another girl into the equation."

"Are you saying I'm a liability? She's my friend too. I'm scared, Felix, and I'm not going to sit at home and hope things turn out okay. I'm coming!"

"Once she's set her mind to it, there's no point trying to convince her otherwise," sighed the blonde—Jasmine's...ex? Girlfriend? Who knew.

"Tamry is right," Jasmine agreed. "Besides, don't count me out of a fight just because I'm a girl. I have three older brothers. I know how to mess a guy up, and Hesper's douchebag father is what, in his fifties? Besides, if your buddy Jackson is built like you, he doesn't stand a chance. Every minute you spend arguing is a minute farther away Hesper is."

Sirens wailed, far off but getting closer.

"Fine. By the time the report is finished Jackson should be here." I winced. I knew his driving, and the hour trip would take him forty minutes tops.

Three officers came in; I wordlessly handed them the piece of Hesper's dress I'd found in the door. It was crumpled from my clenched fist, where I had been unconsciously clinging to it. I told them where to find the bobby pins, and one of them went out to photograph and collect them. It was a frustrating waste of time; this wasn't a mystery. One wanted to ask a few questions; he sat across from me with a pad and a pen, the other standing by the door with his arms crossed, like we were the guilty ones who needed supervision. The questioning bordered on interrogation.

"I'm her *husband*!" I finally burst out indignantly. "I'm the one who noticed she was missing!"

"It's always the husband," Jasmine added sagely while Tamry swatted her arm to make her shut up.

"We literally have video proof it's *not the husband this time*, whose side are you on?" she hissed.

My phone vibrated—a text from Jackson.

"If you'll excuse me," I snapped, "my ride is here, and I'm going to find Hesper." The *even if you won't* was implied.

And why were they lollygagging? Why were they dragging their feet? Because the rest of the security footage had been found, where Ray had dragged my screaming, crying wife across the parking lot and shoved her into the back seat of his car. The college's cameras were good. I could see her beating on the glass of the back window. The vehicle, of course, was Ray's marked Missouri state police squad car—something he could get through roadblocks in, with safety features like a black mesh cage between the front and the back and doors that only opened from the outside.

Even here, even with evidence, the Pennsylvania state troopers were reluctant to go after one of their own. But I was done being patient. I had to get Hesper back. If he made it back to Missouri with her, I might never see her again. Here, they were hesitant to go after him; on his home turf, he was untouchable.

"Get a DVD of the security tapes," Jasmine murmured in Tamry's ear, tucking an errant strand of hair away from her face.

"Will do. You be careful, okay?"

Jasmine's smile was dazzling. "Always, dear." She leaned forward and I suddenly realized why her lipstick was smeared as she kissed her. When she pulled back, Tamry looked starry-eyed and dazed. "I still got it." Jasmine winked and handed her girlfriend her duffel bag. "I'll call you when we're on our way home." She glared at one of the officers. *"With Hesper."*

He opened his mouth to retort, but with her typical dramatic flair, she marched past the man guarding the door and into the night. I went after her before they could stop me, still holding on to Hesper's purse and mask like a life ring. Jackson was leaned against the El Camino waiting. He raised his eyebrows when he saw Jasmine.

"Three to a seat's gonna be a tight squeeze."

"We'll manage," she said airily, breezing past him. "Unless you want me to strap you to the roof, and then we'd only have two to a seat."

I let out a harsh, unexpected bark of laughter at the baffled look on Jackson's face. This was not the reaction he was used to getting—and now two women had shut him down within a couple of months. My hands trembled as I unlocked Calamity's door, and the three of us piled inside on the bench seat.

"This isn't a solid plan," Jackson said doubtfully.

"I don't care. I'm not coming home without Hesper."

I felt his eyes on me, piercing, as I watched the mirrors and backed out of the parking spot.

"You would go to the ends of the earth for this girl. You really meant it when you married her, didn't you?"

Not at the time. I didn't know, didn't understand what I could have, didn't realize it was everything I wanted—what all I was willing to give up in order to have it. It was really about tuition when this whole thing started, about fixing what I had lost instead of realizing what I would gain. I married my best friend before I knew I was in love with her.

"Yes," I agreed for simplicity's sake. "I meant it."

CHAPTER ELEVEN

HESPER

EVENTUALLY I STOPPED screaming. At some point, I just realized it wasn't going to make any difference—nobody was around to hear me. Still, Ray tried to make small talk, and I stared listlessly out of the window. Every time we sped under a streetlamp, I saw the outline of his fingers on my arm, the beginning of bruises blossoming on my skin. When I was sure he wasn't looking, I took off my ring and stealthily stashed it down the front of my dress. I didn't want to give him any more ammunition than he already had.

"You have to talk to me at some point."

"The fuck I do," I hissed.

He hit his brakes hard enough to send me slamming into the cage.

"Language!"

Ray's fingers tightened on the steering wheel. If there wasn't grated metal between us, he'd have reached out and smacked me across the mouth. If there was one thing he hated, it was someone standing up to him.

"I can't believe you were so selfish. Do you know how worried I was when you just up and vanished?"

All I could think of was Felix—how scared he had been the day he came home and couldn't find me. What did he think when I didn't come back from the bathroom? When I had left all my stuff at the table?

"You should have come home. We could have talked it out. You're being unreasonable, but you always have been—too much of your mother in you."

The speedometer crept incrementally higher, closer and closer to ninety. It was a twelve-hour drive going the speed limit, but at this rate we'd make it in eight or nine. It was surprisingly easy to fall back into the silence I grew up with, to tune out his endless chatter. It was less painful. My ears heard it, but my mind was on the pavement stretching out ahead of us, a road ending right back in the hell I thought I'd got out of. Everything he said rolled off my hardened heart, because I knew the truth of it—beneath the guilt trip he was trying to lay on me, there was nothing but rage.

"I don't understand why you wouldn't let me be a part of your life."

Sometimes miles passed between the verbal barrages.

"You're such a spoiled brat. You're so *selfish*."

Sometimes they were one after the other.

"You broke my heart."

All of them were lies.

"I know you're an adult and can make your own choices, but I have no idea what I did that's so terrible it would cause you to turn your back on me and Jo."

That guilt trip worked: when I had run away, I had essentially painted a target on my stepmom's back. If he didn't have me to torment, he would take the next closest thing.

"I put a roof over your head, clothes on your back, and this is how you repay me?"

I didn't dare hum out loud, but I repeated my favorite lyrics over and over in my head, trying to drown him out.

"I tried to leave you alone, thinking you needed some time and you would call. I lay in bed nearly every night wondering what I did to make you turn your back on us."

I counted the light posts on the interstate flashing overhead. I counted my breaths.

"I've spent many nights with little or no sleep just missing you. I've sat and watched videos of you when you were small and sat and cried..."

When he realized he was making no headway—I was present in body but not in spirit—he changed his tactics, knowing laying on guilt and false affection did nothing. I could see right through it. I knew what he was really like.

But he knew where my weakness was.

"As soon as we get home, I've got to get you something to wear. That dress is disgusting."

I picked absently at the skirt, crumpled and torn and ruined now, several scarves missing. I loved my dress. It had made me feel beautiful—which was an entirely new experience. The list of things Ray hated was very long, and most of them included me. He hated women, people who stood up for themselves, anyone who wore anything bigger than a size six. I was all of them, the triple threat that made me a target.

"Have you grown up at all? Still got your head in the clouds?"

I laid down in the seat, staring vacantly at the ceiling, fixating on the roar of the tires, numb to the thirst and exhaustion and the fear and the sinking feeling I had lost it—lost everything, or that everything I had in Pennsylvania was only borrowed, and I should have known I'd lose it eventually. It was never really mine to begin with.

"Randy told me you were married. I thought you didn't like anyone. Maybe now you'll realize how selfish it is not to want children, how much that would hurt your husband. I told you it was a sad, lonely life without kids."

Tears rolled down the sides of my face, but I was careful not to make a sound.

"Who did you marry? Some art school hippie dropout?"

Replying would only let him know he was getting to me. Control was his game. Fear was his power.

"Oh my God," he snapped, disgusted. "Tell me it wasn't that kid you ran off with. The Morlan boy."

I tapped the heel of my sparkly sneaker against the window, wondering what would break first if I tried to kick my way free—my body or the glass.

"You did this just to spite me."

I didn't have my medicine with me. He didn't even know I *took* medicine—that I'd finally gotten help for all the bullshit trauma and resulting mental health issues he'd caused me. No doubt he would mock me for that too.

"You must be ashamed, since you didn't spread the word. You're ruining the Stalides name with that trailer trash—"

The things he had said about me were probably valid—that I was ugly, unloved and unlovable, stupid and broken and disrespectful and generally an unbearable burden. They were things I had always accepted as truth in my heart, despite Felix's insistence my father was just messing with my head.

But Felix. Felix was off-limits.

I snapped.

"Shut up!" I screamed, sitting upright, locking my fingers through the grid of the cage and rattling it. "I ran away for a reason, just leave me alone! I don't ever want to hear his name outta your mouth again!"

I covered my ears and slammed the bottom of my shoe against the back window again and again. It didn't bust. It didn't even crack.

Time had no meaning, trapped in the dark back seat of Ray's squad car. I didn't want to look at the glowing numbers on the dashboard clock. I didn't want to know how long it had been since we had left Morrow, and Felix, and Jasmine, and my art, and my entire future behind us. Several hundred miles had gone by, surely. We had already crossed at least one state line.

Now he'd be able to keep me and my stepmom under one roof, two women under his thumb instead of just one. This would be a power trip of epic proportions. He already saw himself as all-powerful; by taking back the one thing that got away from him, he would be more certain than ever that he was a god.

I let the adrenaline crash and road noise carry me to sleep. Some small part of me—well, less small than usual—hoped I wouldn't wake up. It was the only way this would ever be over.

The dashboard clock read 2:45 when I finally spoke again.

"I have to pee."

"You can hold it."

"Unless you want me staining your back seat, you better pull over."

"I'll make you clean it up when we get home," he threatened, but still got off at the next exit.

We pulled into a twenty-four-hour convenience store and gas station and he turned around.

"Do not say a word to anyone. Go straight in and come straight back out. Do you understand?"

"Yes."

I gritted my teeth, but it was what he wanted to hear. What I had to say to get a shot.

Ray was right on my heels, following so close behind me I could feel his breath on my neck. I made eye contact with the clerk, a girl in her late twenties with a ponytail and dark circles under her eyes, and I tilted my chin up slightly. Maybe she saw the panic in my eyes, because she brushed her hands on her apron and turned to reach for a broom propped in the corner—right by the phone.

I never stopped moving, one foot in front of the other, praying the look on my face had been enough. But as I shut the bathroom door, I saw him whirl around and give his most convincing smile to the clerk, lifting up his jacket to show her his badge. I thumped my head against the door;

my chance was over. His booming voice carried.

"Sorry about that—my daughter...we're from out of state...came to move her back home...just got out of a bad relationship and she's a bit unstable."

I used the bathroom, then ran cold water from the tap and scrubbed the dried tears off my face. It still felt stiff with salt. I couldn't just stay in there, because he'd demand the clerk unlock the door, act sweet and concerned in front of her, and things would be even worse when he got me back into the car. If I started screaming, he'd be able to drive off with me before anyone could come to help. He was bigger and stronger and had spent my whole life bullying me. He was in control and he knew it.

There was an aggressive knock on the door, bordering on banging. As soon as I opened it a sliver, he thrust a plastic shopping bag at me. "Go ahead and put these on."

He had bought a touristy T-shirt a size too small that proclaimed "CROSSROADS OF AMERICA!" like I would be glad to return to the Midwest. A pair of navy sweatpants were shoved in the bottom of the bag. I changed, carefully folded my gala dress—even though he would probably throw it away the first chance he got—and placed it gently in the bag, one last memory from Pennsylvania.

That chapter of my life was probably over now. It didn't hurt as badly as I thought it would—instead, I was numb. I had stolen those three years of freedom, and now I was just paying my dues. I put my ring in my pocket and yanked on the T-shirt neck, though it never seemed to make it any looser or easier to breathe in. The lady at the counter met my eye again, and we had barely made it out the door when I looked over my shoulder and saw her picking up the phone.

He had told her it was fine. Her intuition had told her it wasn't. She was also a girl alone in a store in the middle of the night; she hadn't been able to challenge him directly. Still, she came barreling out of the door once he had shoved me into the back of the squad car, a little breathless.

"Sir, I forgot your change—I can't open the register until my manager gets here with the key. Please come back inside to wait."

Ray narrowed his eyes, sharp and green and cruel. "Keep it."

He got in and slammed the door, ignoring the girl when she tried to convince him to wait. We whipped back onto the road, and onto the interstate. Ray handed me a bottle of water, as a way to keep me occupied and quiet or a reward for not making a break for it—though he genuinely didn't understand what I was so desperate to get away from. He thought this kind of parenthood, ruling with an iron fist, with fear instead of love, was normal. I grew up with the Morlans. I knew better.

"You'll see this is for the best." He had adopted a gentler tone, as if my well-being was really his priority. "You'll live under my roof, under my rules, until you get your head on straight."

"I'm an adult. A grown woman. You can't *make* me stay there."

He shook his head. "Even now you're fighting me. I'm so disappointed in you."

I wanted to pop off that his disappointment didn't hurt me; I had spent my whole life disappointing him, by being born a girl and by every second of my existence since then. I was too mouthy, too impractical, too smart alecky, too stubborn, too fat—too *everything*.

Every second was a battle with myself. I hated fighting and being yelled at. If I went with the flow, I could be the obedient daughter he wanted, trick him into giving me enough freedom to get out from under his thumb again...eventually. However long it took. It could be *years*. And besides, of course he said he would let me go when the time came, but he thrived on controlling others. The truth was, if I tried to compromise, tried to earn the right to be left alone, I would be stuck under his rule forever. I couldn't live with him again, not after knowing what it was like to be free.

My only other option was to keep trying to run, to keep fighting to get back what I'd worked so hard for—peace, freedom, independence, love. A life of my own.

CHAPTER TWELVE

FELIX

THE SUN WAS rising over another state when I woke up, my neck stiff from leaning back against Calamity's passenger window. We had taken to driving in four-hour shifts; I had gone first, stopping in Ohio to swap off with Jackson, who was now snoring softly, his head on my shoulder. Jasmine was at the wheel, her mouth set in a grim line.

"Happy New Year, and welcome to Illinois."

We had made good time. If we were lucky, we had gotten ahead of Ray and we could be there, waiting, when he arrived. If we weren't, he had gotten too much of a head start and was already in Missouri. We'd had the advantage of three drivers; if he had stopped at a hotel for the night, we had hours to prepare. And Hesper's fear of a gunfight be damned, this time the law would get involved and they would take everything from him—his guns, his job, his power, and his freedom. He would go to prison for this. He had to, because it was the only way Hesper would ever be safe. If they could lock up my mom for one stupid decision that ruined her life, they had to prosecute Ray.

They had to. Even if the people arresting him were his coworkers. Even if he knew all the judges. Because he was the bad guy, even when he was hiding behind his badge, and the justice system was supposed to work to protect the innocent.

Right?

"She'll be okay." I wasn't sure if Jasmine was trying to convince herself or me.

"She will," I agreed, but I was terrified because it felt like a lie—the kind you tell yourself because you can't handle the truth.

Jasmine's phone instructed her to take an exit onto another road. Thank God for GPS. I wiggled the phone charger in the semi-functional cigarette lighter, coaxing my phone to hold out until we at least crossed the state line into Missouri. I pulled up my contacts list. We'd lost an hour between time zones, and it was really too early to call, but surely Molly would forgive me this one. Some hard rock song blared—her ringback tone.

"Whooozit?" The sleepy voice of my little sister was faint.

"It's Felix, and I have a really important favor."

"Do you know what time it is?" she complained, but at

least she sounded a little more awake.

"Molls. I left you a car. Work with me here. I need you to do something, but you can*not* tell Dad." This got her attention; shuffling noises crackled from the speaker. I could picture her, wrapped in a duvet with her phone to her ear, trying not to wake Anita in their tiny, shared bedroom. "I just need you to drive by Hesper's dad's house and tell me if his car is parked there—his police car. Can you do that and call me back?"

"Is she okay? Is he bothering her?"

I squeezed my eyes shut. "He took her, and I think they're probably on their way there. They might be there already."

"Holy shit, Felix!"

"Don't! Don't rouse the Morlan Family Alarm. The last thing I need is six angry kids and their only remaining guardian busting down a cop's door. You *know* who'll come out on top of *that* lawsuit."

"We aren't babies anymore, you jerk." Her voice trembled, fear behind her false anger. "But yeah, I'll drive by."

"Thanks. I owe you one. I'm on my way—should be there in..." I tilted Jasmine's phone screen to see the estimated arrival time. "About an hour and a half."

"He was pretty mad when she up and left. Do you think she'll be okay?"

"She'd better be." I didn't finish the threat, letting Molly infer my intentions. "Be careful and call me back."

"Big family?" Jasmine raised an eyebrow, never taking her eyes off the road.

"Huge. Also the best." And I had just sent my baby sister to drive past a monster's house. I cringed.

"What did Jackson mean when he said you meant it when you married Hesper?"

Damn. She didn't miss a trick.

"Are you sure now is the best time to talk about this?"

"I've been driving in complete silence for more than two hours. Name a better time. I'll wait."

"We've been best friends our whole lives—Hesper and I." Her name felt like acid in my throat. "But when we got married, I didn't think I was in love with her."

"This may seem like a fairly obvious question, but why would you marry someone you didn't love?" Her eyes were blazing. "Because it sounds to me like you took advantage of her."

"She's the one who suggested it. It was for convenience. But when I moved in, things changed. I don't know how long I loved her before I finally realized. Honestly? Probably forever. I'm just an idiot who didn't know it, and I was lucky enough I got a chance with her anyway."

"She loves you. Like, for real love. You know that, right?"

"I love her too."

"You better. You might be her best friend, but I care about her, too, and I'll kick your ass if you hurt her."

"Let's get her back safe before we talk about *me* hurting her. I'm not the one she has to be afraid of right now."

"Fair enough."

We had barely gone ten miles before my phone rang. I put Molly on speaker.

"His car is there. The hood is still hot, so they must have just got home."

"You got out of the car? And stood in their driveway?"

"Well, yeah!" she said defensively. "I thought you wanted reconnaissance! Besides, I didn't let anyone see me. It's fine!"

"I did not ask for *recon*." I pinched the bridge of my nose, exhaling as evenly as I could. "Get out of there, Molls. I mean it."

"You want me to sit by while your best friend is held hostage in her dad's basement. Yeah, right."

"Go home and stay put. I'll see you soon."

The landscape changed as we got closer to home, the flat and endless expanses of soybean fields giving way to the hills and trees of Missouri. I hadn't been back since Hesper and I left, headed out east, fresh out of high school setting out on an epic, terrifying, thrilling road trip to a new life. Our old lives were still here though, waiting for us to deal with them.

We pulled into a rest stop for a bathroom break.

"Dude, I get to meet your sisters!" Jackson yawned when I poked him in the ribs, trying to get him out of the seat.

"No."

"What!"

"Don't talk to them. Don't even look at them." Especially not Molly. Jesus Christ, the trouble those two could get into.

He waggled his eyebrows. "I can't stop them from looking at me though."

"Surely there's something in the bro code about this. Besides, I am not letting you hit on my sisters while my wife is in danger! Focus, Jackson!"

He deflated. "Sorry, Felix."

We all swapped seats, and I drove the last thirty miles on autopilot, like some kind of magnet was drawing me home. You could drive straight through Tegan Creek, Missouri and come out the other side in about ten minutes, even taking into account the blinking stoplight at the one intersection dead in the center of town. The first few blocks featured manicured lawns and the houses of affluent families. It was the proverbial white picket fence Midwestern dream, but I passed them, because that wasn't where I was from. I turned left at the intersection, going up a hill and turning left again into a little subdivision. The lots were small and each housed a trailer, separated by patches of tall, scrubby yellow sage grass.

I spotted Molly before I saw home. She was sitting on the trunk of the ancient Accord I had left for her, the bumper held on by bungee cords and a few new dings in the doors. She was in sweatpants and an oversized T-shirt advertising a band I didn't know, her hair piled up on top of her head in a bun and streaked with unexpected pops of bright blue (I was sure Dad had had words with her over that.)

I had hardly gotten Calamity parked in the driveway before she barreled for me, jumped into my arms and laughed as I twirled her, my knee twinging. When she saw Jackson, her eyes got wide. She released me and dropped to the ground, holding her hand out.

"Molly Morlan."

When he reached out to shake it, she fist-bumped him instead. He smiled, not his classic smirk or his smooth, fake grin, and the tightness in my chest eased a little. Sometimes it was easy to forget Molly could give people a run for their money; she was the stubbornest, most spirited person I knew.

"Jackson Maddox."

"I brought backup. Jasmine Miller." I jerked my thumb over to her, where she leaned against the Jeep with her arms crossed, surveying us with interest.

"Awesome mask. When this is all over, think you could teach me?" Molly's eyes gleamed.

"Of course! I might need to wash this off though. Don't want to scare the locals. Got any makeup remover?"

"No problem." My sister turned to me, her arms crossed. "So, what's the plan? If Dad sees you, he'll know something's up, and if you tell him about Hesper, he'll freak."

"Too late for that. When he sees Calamity, he'll know."

The four of us trudged inside. Dad was already sitting at the cluttered kitchen table with a steaming mug of coffee, his salt-and-pepper hair more gray now than black. He had raised seven children; he was no fool, and Molly wasn't nearly as good at sneaking out as she thought she was.

"Happy New Year, Mr. Morlan!" Jackson shouted, as if this would improve the situation.

It did not.

"Dare I ask what brings my eldest home from halfway across the country?" He narrowed his eyes. "Felix Alexander Morlan, is that a wedding ring on your hand?"

Oh, shit.

"Dude, you didn't tell your *dad*?"

I smacked Jackson. *Not helping*, I mouthed.

As I feared, this quickly became a Morlan family meeting. I sat on the kitchen counter with Jackson, Molly sandwiched between us, and Jasmine perched on the end, her feet dangling. My other four sisters and brother trooped in, shepherded by my dad.

He handed me an old, empty glass soda bottle. It was a long-held tradition—whoever held the bottle was the only one allowed to speak. It was how we got through big talks without us all clamoring to be heard over each other. I had never had something quite so big to say as I did now.

They knew about my knee—that my promising athletic career ended before it could ever really start. They knew Hesper let me move in with her after I lost my scholarship and dorm. None of this surprised them. But when I explained our charade—our legally binding contract for free tuition, which eventually turned into a very real, very serious relationship—the bottle code was forgotten. Everyone started talking at once. Jetta, Janie, and Jules all started jumping up and down and screaming. Logan and Anita were shouting, asking questions and demanding answers. The only silent one was Dad, his brows knitted together. I recognized that look. All the puzzle pieces were sliding into place as he remembered my phone call, all the things I didn't tell him then that suddenly made everything else clear.

"Until he passes the bottle off, hush!"

He seldom raised his voice, but when he did, we all listened. Silence fell. Some things I kept to myself—they were between Hesper and me. I left out her struggles with depression, her sexuality, things that just weren't mine to tell. But I did tell them about Ray's steady escalation—letters, phone calls, stalking, breaking in. Abduction was no great leap; we should have seen it coming. When I told them about the video footage proving it was Ray, several of my siblings cringed. All of us knew, for all his outward-facing façade as a good officer and a great man, behind closed doors he was a totally different person. A monster.

"So you already filed a police report. What exactly did you come expecting to do? Burst into his house so he can legally shoot you dead?" Dad glared.

Of course he was right. Missouri had a stand-your-ground law. But here was the truth of it: I had been so focused on getting to her that I had no idea what to do next. Even now, she was probably only a few miles away, but she might as well be on Mars. I hopped off the counter and passed the bottle back to him.

"What do I do?"

"You filed a report. They know he's who took her. They'll get a warrant for his arrest, or at least a search warrant for his home." With every step, Dad counted on his fingers. "They'll arrest him. Then you can go pick up Hesper."

He didn't understand.

"He's a cop, Dad. You really think they're gonna show up and arrest him?"

"Let the law do its job."

"Like it did with Mom?"

The kitchen was deadly silent.

"You know I don't agree with what happened to your mother, but the law's the law. We're all human. She made a mistake—"

"And now she's paying for it for the rest of her life, while we grew up without a mom and assholes like Ray get to do whatever they want! He has never, not once, answered for a single thing he's done!"

"I know you're frustrated. You think I'm happy about a girl I half-raised being kidnapped and held hostage by a man the law won't touch? Of course I'm not! But I think with this"—he tapped his head—"and you think with your temper. You can't help her if you're dead or in jail."

He was right, but I was loath to admit it.

Molly leaned forward on the counter. "Stop fighting! This is the first time we've seen each other in, like, a thousand days. It'll be four years in May. Not exactly how I pictured our grand reunion."

"So, what do you propose we do?" Dad wasn't being mean or sarcastic; he was listening earnestly, his elbows on his knees, slouched over and listening to us. All of us. Just like he always had.

"We just have to wait till Ray goes to work." Logan shrugged.

"But it has to be soon, because we need to document the bruises. Did you see the way he grabbed her on that security footage?" Jasmine was glowering. "If we take her to the police with those bruises and our video evidence, surely we can get something done."

We broke into little clusters, trying to plot our next move. Jackson made no comment about the little trailer I had grown up in, even though his own house was huge. I wasn't ashamed, exactly—everyone had chores and we kept the place spic and span. The fridge was plastered with drawings we had all done in school, even mine, faded and brittle with age. Maybe nobody had their own bedrooms, but our house was full of love, and that was somehow more important than all the things Jackson had that I never would.

He handled it very tactfully, surprisingly—I had known him for several years, had lived with him for most of it, and sensitivity wasn't usually his strong suit. I left them all chattering in the kitchen to raid Logan's closet. He had grown so much since I left, and I gratefully stole a T-shirt that was almost my size and a pair of jeans that fit okay. I hung up my borrowed suit. The gala felt like weeks ago; it was just last night. Everything was surreal, right down to the nine other people packed into our tiny kitchen like sardines. My life in Pennsylvania and my life in Missouri, crammed into one space.

"Didja find something that fits?"

Logan was standing in the doorway, looking troubled. He was still in pajama pants, his cowlicks sticking up all over the place, and I saw him both as my little brother and an almost-adult. It was disconcerting, nostalgic, a tangle of feelings I didn't expect.

"Yeah. Thanks. I promise I'll get them back to you before I leave."

"So you're just here to get Hesper back." He leaned against the jamb. "Not, like, to stay. Which I should have known, since you brought your friends."

"Do you—do you *want* me to stay?" I asked, surprised.

"Of course I do. The house is full of girls. Plus, I just miss you." He looked embarrassed, ducking his head. "Which is dumb, I guess. We're grown-ups now, and I *do* like having a room to myself. But hanging out with Molly and Anita isn't like hanging out with you."

My chest ached. He wasn't a grown-up quite yet. He had just celebrated his sixteenth birthday. Still, he saw it as us versus them, the two Morlan boys against the five Morlan girls—and I didn't realize how much would fall on his shoulders when I left. Dad worked two jobs. That meant Logan was usually the *only* guy in the house. He felt responsible for the rest of them, when he should have just had time to be a kid.

"My classes don't start for another two weeks. And besides, we'll probably be tied up with police reports here for a while. I promise we'll hang out."

"I hope Hesper's okay. She's like family, y'know?" He made a face, crinkling up his nose. "*Actually* family. I guess she's my sister-in-law now. You know Anita and Molly have had a running bet since you two were freshmen, right?"

"Oh my God! How did everyone know except the two people in the actual relationship!"

"Don't hold your breath; pretty sure Hesper knew too. Did you really not see it?"

No. I hadn't. Not until it fell into my lap.

"Pizza's here!" Jackson bellowed from the kitchen.

It was far too early for pizza. None of us cared. We dragged chairs in from other rooms, an odd hodgepodge of furniture crammed around the table. Jackson had ordered, and discreetly paid for, four large pizzas, which all sat open in the center of the table. We ate over napkins, my family and my friends and me. If Hesper was there, I'd go dig in the refrigerator to see if we had any banana pepper rings for her pizza. I'd sit her on my lap, and we'd eat lunch while I told her the best (worst?) puns.

This was not forever. We would get her back, and then we could have this for real.

"I'M NOT USING you as bait."

We sat in the living room, more or less in a circle on the

floor, planning. Well, trying to plan, if Molly would stop firing off bad, dangerous ideas. She had rather gleefully suggested causing mayhem somewhere on the Stalides property, everything from tagging the storage shed behind the house to taking a baseball bat to Ray's personal vehicle, a big white SUV that cost as much as a house.

"But it'll lure him out!"

"No!" Luckily, Dad was still the voice of reason. "No law-breaking! No illegal shenanigans!"

"But shenanigans are my specialty." She grinned.

"He'll have to go to work eventually."

"Nobody is gonna set foot on that property but me," I interrupted. "I half grew up there, and I know my way around inside and out. He has an alarm system on the front and back doors, or he used to. Hesper didn't know the code, so I don't. My only shot is sneaking through a window."

"We'll listen to the scanner and keep you posted," Molly volunteered. "We'll call in an anonymous tip to the district headquarters that he's wanted in Pennsylvania. Even if they insist it's a misunderstanding, they'll at least call him in to explain and that should buy you some time."

"You guys have a police scanner? In your house?" Jackson looked puzzled. Apparently, this was a Midwest thing; Jasmine looked baffled as well.

"Everyone does."

He seemed to take Molly's word for it, nodding sagely like it suddenly made sense to him.

I hovered at the edge of the door, Jackson and Jasmine behind me, while Molly sat on the saggy living room sofa and spoke in a low, urgent voice. She used Jasmine's phone to make the call so it would show up as a Pennsylvania cell number.

Ray's district office was a twenty-minute drive each way. Even if he sped—he *always* sped—and was only detained a few minutes, that bought us at least half an hour. The sun was setting. We got one clean run at this, and if we blew it, we'd have to think of something else...while hoping the Stalideses didn't press trespassing charges if we were busted.

Once we heard his sergeant call him out, the three of us set out on foot, back down the road we had driven in on. I had walked the path between our houses hundreds, probably thousands of times growing up—every day in the summer, and most days after school. She would come to my house on Saturday mornings, lie in a pile on the floor with my sisters, and watch cartoons.

So many years, and so much had changed. When we finally got out of here after high school, I thought I had walked this path for the last time. We trooped to the farthest edge of town, where neighbors were few and far between but the houses were well-built with expensive trucks in the driveways. I couldn't let anyone see Calamity and I didn't want to risk the noise of her engine. Jasmine and Jackson stood back beyond the edge of Ray's yard, waiting for trouble in case I needed backup.

It was a split-level, with a basement floor emerging from the hill the house was built into on the back side. The plum tree on the west side by the front porch was nothing but a scraggly bunch of branches reaching for the sky, the leaves having long since fallen.

The leaves leave in the winter, I imagined whispering to Hesper. (*Oh my God, Felix, I want a divorce,* she would laugh. I would want to kiss her but would settle for holding her while she struggled to look stern and disapproving.) I crept over to the window by the plum tree and peered in to see it was painted yellow now, filled with police memorabilia, a defunct tanning bed, and piles of travel books. The colors and contents of the room had changed, but the layout was still the same. I could walk this entire house in my sleep.

I slotted my fingers under the sash and heaved. It wasn't made to be opened from that side, and it groaned and skittered up a few notches, just enough to slide my fingers through and push it open. I climbed through the window, awkward and entirely too tall. I had to give Molly credit—it was harder than it looked in the movies, and I bit down on my tongue, stifling a groan when I landed on my bad knee.

Hesper's room was downstairs. I peered around the corner into the long hallway, spotting her stepmom at the table, her face blotchy and resting in her hand, an old cordless phone tucked between her ear and shoulder. When she reached for a box of tissues, I slipped out and made a break for the carpeted basement stairs, my heart hammering in my ears. She honked loudly, her voice growing louder and more hysterical on the phone, and *surely she didn't see me*.

At the bottom of the stairs, the hall split—the garage to the right, a locked door to the left.

In addition to the regular doorknob lock, a dead bolt had been installed.

I checked my phone. According to the original timeline I still had ten minutes left—but I also had a text from Molly. Ray had gone off the air after his meeting with his sergeant, which had been briefer than we feared, and he sounded furious. I had, at best, five minutes. I unlocked the door to the rest of the basement, then the door off to the right—Hesper's room—and threw it open. I don't know what I was expecting...maybe for her to jump into my arms, that I would carry her out of the door to safety and we'd run and never look back. But she didn't even know I was there.

When she left, they must have converted her bedroom to a rec room—no bed, no dresser, just a ping-pong table and a few beanbag chairs. The walls were still the same blue-lavender as they had always been though. And there, listless and curled up on the floor, clutching her ruined purple dress and wearing clothes that didn't belong to her, was my best friend.

My girlfriend.

My wife.

Hesper.

CHAPTER THIRTEEN

HESPER

THE CEILING TILES were brown with water stains, the room musty with disuse. There was nothing to pick the lock with, nothing to read, nothing to write on. But at least Ray was gone for the time being. When I was a kid, I did my best to sleep as much as I could when I was in this house, because then my mind wouldn't loop all the horrible things he said over and over. It was my escape.

Turned out it still worked. It was an old trick, but a useful one. I constantly floated in and out of sleep, caught in that weird in-between place where everything seemed empty and quiet.

"Hesper."

I closed my eyes.

"Hesper!"

It wasn't Ray's voice.

A sturdy pair of arms slid under me to lift me up, and I immediately started fighting, shoving with my free hand and holding the purple fabric bunched in my other one closer to my chest, kicking and flailing and opening my mouth to scream—

"Stop that, we gotta hurry."

It clicked.

"Felix."

He put me down, making sure I was capable of standing on my own. My legs were wobbly and sore, but they held me.

There was no overwhelming rush of emotions. I had turned myself off and didn't know how to boot back up again. But maybe the numbness was good, at least for now— I couldn't afford to break down. He kept an arm around my waist to hold me steady, and the sensation of it—being close to him—started to fracture the layer of frost over my feelings. Out of the door to the stairs, through the garage.

Felix whispered in my ear. "We need to get out of here, pronto."

Out through the back door and into the chilly evening air. The gravel in the front driveway popped as Ray's squad car tore in and came screaming to a stop. We made a break for the trees. We'd find our way out of the woods if we had to—we just had to get away from that house. Besides, how many hours had we spent playing there? It had to have been hundreds, thousands. The fort we built with fallen branches was probably still somewhere inside.

There was no foliage on the trees to hide us, the branches scraped at our skin, and the leaf litter crunched too loudly beneath our feet, threatening to give us away if we were being pursued, and I tripped and Felix tried to catch me and we both fell, a tangle of arms and legs. We didn't get up right away, straining our ears for other footsteps, for shouting if my absence had been discovered.

"How do you find your way to a New Year's party?" Felix whispered, his breath warming the skin of my neck, waiting a beat before adding, "By following the Auld Lang *sign*."

I couldn't help it—I laughed, and it broke something loose in me, clinging to him in the cold dark of the woods, lying in the dirt and the leaves, but free. He rubbed my back, whispering things I could only catch snatches of—*love* and *thank God* and *lost you*. The first sob rattled loose, and he crushed me to his chest, the dial tone of a phone audible.

"We're in the woods behind the house. Call the police. I'm not moving with her...yes, I've got her."

I heard Jackson and Jasmine screaming on the other end.

They had crossed the country. They had come with Felix. They had saved me. Felix's hands were steady on my shoulder blades, consoling me, and all I could hear was my own ugly sobbing and gasping breaths and a brand-new roar of panic.

Police.

"No! No, no police," I begged, clutching my fists in his shirt. "He's one of them, he's—"

"Hesper, no. Hesper. Breathe."

I didn't want to breathe. I wanted to get back up and start running and never, ever stop. Pennsylvania wasn't far enough. I'd change my name, I'd change my face, I'd disappear and they'd never find me again.

"Listen to me!" He tried to keep me still; I was shaking. I couldn't stop. "Listen. This will go on forever unless we stop it. The only way to make sure this never happens again is to make this stick. If we can't get charges here, we'll try in Pennsylvania—"

"No!" I tried to squirm away from him, but he held me fast. "No trials, I can't testify—"

"You *can*, Hesper."

I sobbed, bringing my fists down ineffectually on his chest. "I'm so fucking scared, Felix."

"Everyone is scared. This is our first real shot at getting him convicted though."

"They won't! They won't, he gets away with everything."

The sirens were getting closer, and if they tried to arrest him or take him in for questioning—

"He'll kill them," I sobbed. "The officers and Jo. He'll kill them all before he'll let it end. It'll never be over."

His grasp slipped just long enough for me to get loose. I staggered to my feet and didn't stop, taking in great gulps of freezing air and stumbling over rocks and sticks and tangled snarls of weedy vines.

Free.

Free.

Free.

Someone came crashing after me at a pace Felix couldn't manage with his knee, and I pumped my arms, putting on an extra burst of speed, my lungs burning. I would never stop. Nothing could ever make me stop.

"Hesper!"

Thick, heavily muscled arms locked around me like a vise and lifted me up off the ground while my legs pedaled helplessly. I howled. They wouldn't let me go.

"Pull it together!" It was Jackson. He gave me a little shake. "I've got you. You think we drove halfway 'cross the United States just to let that asshole hurt you again? Naw. You're safe."

But I wasn't. Safety was an illusion, a lie I'd let myself believe for three years and look where it got me.

"I'll never be safe. Never," I sobbed.

The panic though, was starting to drain away. I went limp. I stopped fighting. Running would accomplish nothing. It felt necessary, it felt like I needed to keep moving and never stop, but where would that get me? I couldn't keep it up forever. I couldn't start again somewhere new. The life I fought so hard for was still waiting for me in Pennsylvania. My job, Zach, my house, Morrow—the blossoming relationship I had begun with Felix.

Felix, who chased me all the way back here and risked everything to get me back. Who I left lying on the ground, when he had probably already reinjured his knee trying to get me somewhere safe. I thought I had no tears left, that I had used up all my self-loathing.

I was wrong.

"Hey, hey, hey," Jackson murmured. He had no idea how to deal with a crying girl. "Uh, stop? You're okay now. I gotcha."

I struggled weakly again.

"If I put you down, are you gonna run again?"

"No."

"You better not." He gingerly set me back on my feet,

but kept one hand on my shoulder just in case.

Felix was shambling toward us, favoring his knee, the brace on the outside of his jeans straining against the swelling. The three of us trooped toward the sound of the sirens, one man on each side of me, ready to help me if I fell or catch me if my panic got a hold of me again. But it wouldn't. I would be brave. I had to be.

If I wanted my life back, I had to fight for it...and fight for everyone else he had terrorized, would continue to terrorize unless someone stopped him.

And it was me. It had to be me. I had bruises all up my arms in the shape of his hands. Surely to God, this time people would believe me. They couldn't deny the proof, even if he was a pillar of the community.

Jasmine was talking animatedly, glaring at the officer she had cornered. They were standing by one of the patrol cars, which was throwing blue and red lights through the trees. It was the county police, not the state, so the bias would be less obvious...but I didn't trust them. How could I? He was one of them.

"I need to give a voluntary statement." My voice was bolder, louder than I expected. "And report unlawful restraint."

The officer raised an eyebrow, surprised I knew the lingo. "Do you need medical treatment?"

"No. I just need to document these." I shoved my arms out, deep purple standing out on the pale undersides. "And I need you to match them to the culprit."

"And an abduction—" Jasmine started to argue.

"No. The abduction charge will be in Pennsylvania." I fought against the reflex to heave. There would be more than one court case—more than one charge. I would have to relive every second since the gala on the witness stand, *twice*. If they didn't dismiss it before it ever went to court. If he didn't grow tired of the game and just kill me first.

Everyone thought that was dramatic. An exaggeration. But they hadn't lived with him. They didn't know the truth. I could point to every patched-over spot in the drywall he had punched through before.

Felix wrapped an arm around me, holding me steady.

"You're okay now." The officer—his collar brass said Jeffries—tried to usher me into the back seat of his car.

The impulse was immediate. If Felix hadn't had such a good grip, I'd have turned tail again.

"No no no no." It all came out in one breath.

There was no cage. The doors would not be locked. I would be free to go at any time. But going into that car felt like walking right back into a nightmare. Felix tossed keys—my keys, Calamity's keys—to Jasmine.

"I'm riding with her. Meet us there." He climbed into the back seat and held out his hand.

"Sir—"

"She is my wife," he cut off the policeman with a glare. "And I am going with her."

Jeffries nodded, and the knot in my chest eased. Felix had driven nine hundred miles to spring me out of this mess, and if he could get in, so could I. The officer shut the door gently, but the sound still made me cringe. We pulled away as another policeman knocked on Ray's front door. Even with the windows up, the screaming was audible.

"You've gotta be kidding me. I won't entertain such a ridiculous thing. This is a misunderstanding! My daughter is just mad at me—"

We rounded the corner and passed several more cars on their way to assist. They should have waited until Jo was safe. They should have waited until he had no access to weapons. They should have waited until I was out of earshot, at least, before he started screaming his head off about how this was all my fault, that I was a petulant child throwing a tantrum, that he was the betrayed victim and I was the monster.

He had been spreading that lie for three years in my absence. Why would they believe me over him? To all outward appearances, he was a fine, upstanding man, an officer of the law with a beautiful wife. I really did look like the villain here. And here I was about to go tell his peers that he had loaded me up in his police car, hauled me across the country, tried to extort obedient behavior for my freedom, and held me captive in his basement.

"Breathe," Felix whispered in my ear. "You're spiraling. Don't panic. It will be okay."

"What makes you think it'll be okay?"

He held out his hand—offering to let me hold it if I needed, ready to let it drop if I couldn't handle it. The first tear trickled down my face, but he didn't wipe it away. He let me cry, because it was what I needed, a way to release all that pent-up emotion. I grabbed his fingers so tight he should have pulled away, but he didn't, just squeezed back in a slow and steady rhythm that I timed my breaths around.

"Don't forget to breathe," he murmured, "but it's okay to cry. It's fine to feel the way you're feeling, but you're safe, okay?"

There were bags under his eyes, two dark-purple half-moons. Had he slept at all since the gala? It wasn't so long ago, but felt like a lifetime, a monumental split that divided my life into before when everything was fine, and afterward when nothing would ever be fine again. Maybe he needed the comfort as much as I did, but I had no way to give it to him.

"This is where I'd tell you a pun, if I knew any."

This took him off guard, eliciting a startled laugh. "I'll teach you some when we get home."

I stared out of the window at the houses we passed, getting closer to the county police department. "We'll never get home."

"As long as we're together, we're always home, Hes. My home is where you are." He leaned his head over on mine, and I closed my eyes, still inhaling and exhaling to the rhythm of his hand tightening and easing.

Jeffries pulled around to the back. He was young, closer to my age than Ray's, and pale, his blue eyes enormous when he caught sight of my arms again. I tugged on the sleeves of my too-tight T-shirt self-consciously.

"They're going to be bringing in...ah...the accused." He didn't seem to want to say Ray's name. "I don't want him seeing you, so if you'll follow me—"

"I need to file a restraining order. It won't make a difference, because he thinks he's above the law—" Jeffries's ears went pink at this, but I continued anyway, louder. "—but I want it in writing that he can't be near me, and he can't have his guns."

"There's a victim's advocate inside." He opened the door and I sprung out as fast as I could, taking in great gulps of cold, fresh night air. "She'll help you with that paperwork.

I need to take photographs of..." He gestured toward my arms.

The three of us walked single file down a musty-smelling hallway with dark paneled walls and old gray carpet. A dehumidifier hummed somewhere close by. Jeffries made Felix wait outside the door of a cramped little office.

"Did he have anything to do with this?" he asked softly.

"What? No!"

"Domestic violence—"

"I appreciate what you're trying to do here, but I know who attacked me. You're not gonna want to hear it though."

He held his hands up. "I'm sorry. I just want to do this right and give you every opportunity to tell me anything that might be going on." He slid a pad across the desk, a pen balanced on top. "Your voluntary statement."

I held the pen over the paper while he rummaged around in a drawer and pulled out a camera with a neck strap. I was poised on the edge of a cliff, and once I jumped, there was no going back. Where did I even start? Before the gala, he sent letters, he called and harassed me. Before I moved out to Pennsylvania, he spent his whole damn life making me feel stupid and ugly and weak and unlovable and inadequate. So I told it from the beginning, filling up one page, two pages, my hand cramping as I continued to write and write and write. I only stopped to hold out my arms for Jeffries to take photographs of every finger-shaped bruise. My face was also turning a delicate shade of purple where I'd slammed into the cage in the back of Ray's car.

Jeffries got a text message, and he rushed over to the door while I filled up my fifth and final page and cracked it just enough to allow Felix to slip in.

"I don't have a single police joke," he murmured in my ear, and I laughed despite myself. "What a tragedy."

He pulled his chair right up next to mine, the sides touching. I reached over, my hand hovering inches away from his face, and he nodded. His cheek was stubbly under my fingers, my thumb tracing gently across his sharp cheekbone.

I heard a voice, getting louder as its owner approached up the hall, and it took all my self-control to sit still. My fight-or-flight reflex was vibrating, urging me to do something, anything.

"You know how kids are. I went and got her out of a bad situation—"

"Even though she did you wrong," another man grumbled. "I haven't forgotten how she broke your heart when she left here."

"But she's my daughter. I just want what's best for her." Ray's voice was oily, saccharine and terrible. "And this is how she repays me."

"We have to investigate though, to cover our asses."

"And charge her with filing a false police report when it comes up nothing." Ray's voice was fading as they passed, getting farther away with every step.

Jeffries looked at me with wide, lamp-like eyes. Felix took my hand from his face and kissed my knuckles, his expression troubled. A miserable understanding passed between the three of us. It was us versus them; the girl who was a pariah in town, the rookie policeman, and the failed football star versus the respected cop and the veteran officers who worked with him. We didn't stand a chance. We were already the losers here.

Nobody would believe me, because nobody ever did... unless I could get Jo on my side. We would stand a chance if I could convince her it was more dangerous to stay than it was to stand up and fight. If I got an order of protection against him, they would take away his guns, potentially his job, and definitely his standing in the community. He would have nothing to lose.

Nothing was scarier than a man like him with nothing to lose.

"I need to see a judge and file an emergency order."

"It's New Year's Day."

"I don't care." I leaned forward, gathering all the steel in me and trying to sound confident, determined, with no room for argument. "I have been abducted, threatened, dragged halfway across the country, and locked in a room. The only time I was let out was for bathroom breaks—and those were supervised. Forgive me if I'm not willing to take the chance that it'll happen again."

If Jasmine was here, she'd punch my shoulder and yell, *get 'em, girl*! Even Felix looked impressed. Because if I'd grown a backbone and stood up to him instead of running away the first time, none of this would have happened. I would take whatever steps, whatever risks I had to in order to make sure he would never hurt anyone again.

THIS WASN'T HOW I expected to be reunited with Felix's family. I parked Calamity in their driveway like I had a thousand times before, and Morlans came spilling out of the doorway, Molly in front. I barely managed to get out of the

Jeep before she reached out and grabbed me. They had always been the reluctant exception to my no-touching rule, because that was simply how they were—rambunctious, affectionate, loud and messy and wild.

"Thank God!" she exclaimed, squeezing me like a doll. She was almost Felix's height, long and thin but incredibly strong. "Felix called this morning and scared the shit out of me!"

"Watch your mouth," Mr. Morlan warned, but he smiled warmly at me, taking his turn to hug me.

Anita and Logan stood back, smiling, a little more understanding of my issues with human contact, but the three youngest—Janie, Jules, and Jetta—barreled at me, shrieking and throwing themselves at me so hard the four of us almost tumbled to the ground, all talking at once.

"We miss you so much!"

"Molly never braids our hair like you did, can you do mine?"

"You're our sister now!"

"Sister-in-*law*," one corrected, and the first stuck her tongue out in response.

"What*ever*," she sniffed.

I raised an eyebrow at Felix. Clearly the cat was out of the bag. He smiled sheepishly at me, holding his hand up. His ring was still on his finger. I took mine out of my pocket and slipped it on. I knew his body language—he leaned toward me, his eyes full of something I didn't, couldn't, understand or reciprocate. He wanted to kiss me. I still couldn't let him. I swallowed, looking away, and the moment was lost. He curled his hand around my waist and pulled me into his side, out from under the pile of Morlan girls who were hanging off me, one on each elbow and one with her arms around my neck.

"Nice hair," I commented to Molly, surprised to find I could muster a grin. I must have cried myself out.

"Thanks!" She patted the bun on her head fondly, a knot of brown streaked with electric blue. "I'm a fan, though I think I might go pink next time."

"Next time?" Mr. Morlan squawked, but she ignored him.

It made me want to draw her, and for the first time, I felt almost normal again. I reached into the little storage compartment behind Calamity's driver's seat and grabbed my go-bag with emergency art supplies—the same one I had taken into the hospital when Felix suffered his injury. It felt like a lifetime ago.

I wanted my little painting closet under the stairs.

I wanted our bedroom, our bed—because it wasn't really mine anymore. I couldn't imagine it without Felix in it with me.

I wanted to run away, go home, pretend like this was all just a bad dream.

And maybe it would be, if I fought hard enough. If this time, I won.

"I need my phone. Did you bring it?"

The herd of Morlans retreated into their trailer while I leaned against Calamity's bumper, star-sixty-sevening my number so I could hang up quick if I needed and nobody could redial. I half expected it to be Ray who picked up. Maybe he was still at the station though, because it was Jo's wary voice on the other end of the line.

"Hello?" she asked cautiously.

I clutched my cell. In a different world, we could have been friends—she was closer to my age than Ray's.

"Don't hang up," I begged. It would be her first impulse. I had left her behind to deal with his wrath not once, but twice now. "It's Hesper."

I expected her anger, but it wasn't there, just a sad, tired sort of acceptance.

"What do you want?"

"To warn you that I filed an emergency order of protection against him...and to beg you to leave. Please."

"I'm already ahead of you. I'm packing my bags now. I'm going to my parents' house to ride this out."

"Don't ride it out. It'll never get better."

She was quiet for a long time. "You know how he is about control. He'll hurt me if I try to leave."

"Not if he's in prison."

"He'll never go to prison."

"He deserves to."

"He never gets what he deserves." She started crying, sniffling, her voice jagged and broken. "Why couldn't you just do what he asked? Why did you drag his name through the mud? He's not so hard to live with as long as you give him what he wants."

My fraying temper snapped. I wasn't just angry, I was scared—scared she wouldn't be on my side, scared of what Ray would do to all of us if this mutiny failed.

"None of us should have to be afraid all the time. He gets away with everything. It's gotta stop! You think it'll end with me?" I slammed my fist down on Calamity's hood. "He'll never quit hurting people, and things are about to get a whole lot worse."

"What do you want me to do about it?"

"The same thing I did—stand up to him. I know it's terrifying. But if we both testify, we stand a chance at starting over. Of being free."

She wasn't even forty yet. She could still move on, have a life. I could go home and figure myself out, figure out how Felix and I could work on building a new life out of the ashes of our old ones.

"Call me later." Her voice trembled. "I'm going to talk to my mom."

The line went dead.

CHAPTER FOURTEEN

FELIX

I NEVER WOULD have dreamed we'd have another New Year's sleepover in my living room, but there we were. Well after midnight, Jasmine curled up on the couch, and Jackson stretched out by the heating vent, snoring softly in a spare blanket I recognized, belatedly, as Molly's. I'd have to give him a Talk in the morning (not that it would stop them; they got on like a house fire, he acted mostly respectable around her, and God help anyone who tried to tell my sister what to do.)

As for Hesper and me, we laid out on a pallet of blankets on the floor. I wanted to crush her to me, to hear her heartbeat and feel her safe and sound, but her face and arms were swollen and varying shades of blue and purple and I was half-afraid to touch her. She was so strong in some ways but so fragile in others, like she'd break apart at the seams. It was taking everything she had to lie beside me, not to go outside, get in Calamity, start driving and never come back. She wanted to run forever—and how could I blame her for that? Our fingers were knitted together in the darkness, the only contact we dared to make.

When I looked at her bruises, I didn't want to go to court and wait for the law to wind its slow path to justice. I wanted to fucking kill Ray. I wanted Hesper to be safe.

"I called Zach to let him know you're okay. He knows where your spare key is hidden and he's gonna overnight your medicine."

Her breathing was low and even, but she squeezed my hand to let me know she heard and understood. She didn't thank me, but I felt the gratitude in the spasm of her fingers. One less phone call to make was always a good thing for her.

"I don't want to go to sleep." Her voice was so faint I could barely hear her. "My nightmares can be...loud."

I gently ran my thumb across her knuckles. "Nobody will hold it against you. I'd be worried if you *didn't* have nightmares after that."

It was a long time before she spoke again. "I'm sorry I ran from you in the woods."

Her voice, her sobs, *I'm so fucking scared*—it played on loop, in my ears, in rhythm with the blood rushing through my veins. I couldn't let the rage creep into my voice; I couldn't let her think it was directed at her. I chose my words deliberately.

"It wasn't me you were running from."

She rolled over, wincing, the soft curve of her face illuminated by the moonlight shining in through the living room window. She had two black eyes, but the damage ran deeper than that. Deeper than her skin. Her eyes were wide, flat, and hollow.

"It's killing me to sit still. To just...wait on him to get away with it and get me again."

"I'll never let that happen."

Her teeth chattered, visible in the tremor of her jaw. "I'm not brave enough for this."

"You don't have to be brave. Of course you're scared. I'm scared too." I swallowed, the words taking up too much room in my mouth. "But I'm with you, H."

She held out one arm tentatively, half permission, half request. When I nodded, she burrowed against me, her head against my shoulder, and I tucked my arms around her. She shook with fear and grief and oh, God, I'd kill him for doing this to her. I curled one hand against the back of her head, smoothing down her hair.

"Here's what we'll do: the emergency order of protection was granted. The hearing for a...a...whatever it's called—"

"Plenary," she supplied.

"A *plenary* order is in two weeks. We stay until then. When it's granted—"

"—if it's granted—"

"—we go home and tackle this on our own turf." I remembered what she said to me when I was the hopeless one, scared and confused and facing an uncertain future. The word I needed to hear the most, to let me know she had my back. "Together?"

She pressed her lips to my cheek, a ghost of sensation there and gone again. "Together."

I ran my thumb across the band on my left ring finger, thinking of the weight of *together*, of the girl in my arms and friends who'd driven halfway across the country with me to keep her safe. I lay there in the dark and listened to the sounds of the house I grew up in, waiting for the slam of heavy fists on the door or an unfamiliar creak signaling someone else was in the house with us.

THE NEXT MORNING, I woke up to the buttery smell of frozen waffles fresh from the toaster. Jasmine and Molly were settled cross-legged on the couch, wearing white pore strips on their noses and looking at makeup brushes on their phones, their heads bent together. Jackson, for his part, listened raptly, as if he gave a single crap about budget beauty routines.

When I reached out, my fingers brushed cool, empty sheets. Hesper wasn't in our makeshift bed.

If I went outside, would Calamity be gone? I sat up so fast my head spun.

"Calm yourself, pun boy." Jasmine had her arms crossed, offering me a smile. "She's in the kitchen helping your brother on the waffle assembly line. In case you haven't noticed, you have a small army to feed."

I picked up my phone and texted her.

9:26 AM

What do you call a waffle on

a beach?

I waited a beat for her phone to go off.
"*Felix!*"
I laughed in relief at the sound of her voice from the kitchen, her mock frustration comfortingly familiar.

9:26 AM

A SANDY EGGO

9:27 AM

Get it?

9:27 AM

Like San Diego?

Hesper stormed into the living room, waving her phone animatedly.

"I thought you wanted me to teach you some puns!"

"Oh, I never should have said that."

The chagrin on her face made me smile like an idiot, warmth spreading through my chest. Her hair was in a messy braid and she wore a pair of basketball shorts and a T-shirt Logan had gotten too tall for, and despite her bruises she looked fierce and beautiful and I wished so desperately that I could kiss her.

She brandished a bottle of squeeze butter at me, and I held up my hands in surrender.

The moment was broken by three hard knocks on the door. To Hesper's credit, she didn't bolt, just held perfectly still, frozen in place with wide eyes. I had never seen the color go from her face so fast. Jackson wordlessly reached down and helped me to my feet but I still staggered, my knee aching like a bitch from the tumble we took in the woods the night before. Molly held up her phone, her face pinched in anger.

"Want me to call 9-1-1?"

I gently pushed past Hesper and made for the kitchen door when the knock sounded again. Anita shepherded Jetta, Janie, and Jules into their room. Logan exchanged a wide-eyed look with me, his hair sticking up and his feet bare and looking so impossibly *young*. I swung open the door, Jackson at one shoulder and my brother at the other, but Ray was already gone, his SUV throwing gravel as he jammed his foot on the accelerator.

There was a piece of paper under Calamity's windshield wipers, and I strode outside into the frigid January morning, not feeling one bit of the cold, hands shaking. I yanked the letter from the glass so violently it almost ripped in two. It was typed, not written; of course it was. Of course he wouldn't put his handwriting on it. And if we tried to say he left it there, he'd insist we printed it out and planted it. Because that's the kind of jackass he was.

Hesper's face was a pale smudge in the doorway, but as I approached she didn't shy away. Her hands were steadier than mine as she pried the letter from me.

It was none of my business. She had every right to read it, but I also didn't want it to hurt her.

Her jaw clenched as she read it. Nobody would meet her eyes. She handed it back to me and returned calmly to the sink. She stuck her arms into the dishwater and scrubbed at syrup-sticky mismatched plates and forks. The room slowly came back to life around her, everyone moving tentatively, half-expecting some sort of reaction. Logan leaned against the counter beside her and began shoveling forkfuls of waffle into his mouth.

"Do you want to talk about it?"

"There's nothing to talk about. He's on suspension at work, I've ruined his reputation, I'm a horrible, ungrateful daughter. I should be thankful he put a roof over my head for so many years, and he can't believe this is how I've repaid him." Her tone was neutral, her shoulders set—every word was matter-of-fact. "The same crap he always says. He wants me to drop the order and rescind my statement. I won't. I'm done letting him control me."

She was afraid—I saw the impulse to bolt barely held in check, the effort it took her to feign nonchalance. But fear was how Ray kept his thumb on her for so many years. By refusing to back down, she was taking his power away.

I had spent my whole life being proud of her. Proud of her art, her grades, her indomitable spirit—the way that, no matter how hard life kicked her feet out from under her, no matter her inner demons whispering that she should just stay down, she always had the strength to get back up. But this was something else, something so much bigger.

"Stop looking at me like that." She tried to sound cross, but her voice cracked. "Like I'm glass. Like I'm about to break."

"I know you won't. You're the strongest person I know." I handed her a dish towel—worn thin from use, but it was one of Mom's, and none of us could quite bear to part with it—and she dried her hands. "But if you need to, that's okay too. Because I'll always be here to help you put yourself back together."

Her eyes widened momentarily in surprise, then she smiled a smile that would have knocked me flat. I didn't need to kiss her, or even touch her. I just needed her to look at me like that, like she felt seen and understood. That was enough.

"You're ridiculous," she muttered.

I grinned. "I'm the best husband ever, you say? Because that's what I heard."

"That too." We were toe to toe now, her head tilted back slightly to look me in the eye.

Logan made a gagging noise. "I'm out. Y'all have ruined my appetite."

I reached out and ruffled his hair. He batted at me irritably, but I didn't miss the way he leaned into my touch. I grabbed him in a bear hug.

"Get off me!"

Anita threw her arms around us both in solidarity, and for all his complaints, Logan didn't even squirm.

"Group hug without me?" Molly sounded appalled and piled on, and Janie, Jetta, and Jules all flooded back in and bickered loudly as they tried to squeeze in and suddenly I was in the middle of the cluster, surrounded by my siblings.

"You're a wimp," Logan said fondly, pulling his arm loose and wiping his hand roughly against my face. It was wet. When had I started crying?

He sniffled too though.

There was one reunion I still needed to have, one person I hadn't seen yet. One person who still didn't know...anything that had happened in the three years since I left, who needed to know about Hesper and me.

"I've…got somewhere to go."

Jackson looked at me over the heap of Morlans—coming through in the clutch as always. (*Maybe* it wasn't the end of the world that Molly was making eyes at him.)

"Need company?"

"No. I won't be gone long."

I raised an eyebrow at Hesper. Maybe I'd bring her with me for the next visit, but this was one I needed to do alone.

"I'll be fine." She rolled her eyes at my unspoken question. "I *am* capable of functioning on my own."

"If Ray comes back, call 9-1-1. Coming here violates the order of protection." I smiled grimly. "And if he does that, he can be arrested. Can I borrow Calamity?"

She tossed me her keys. "Marital property, y'know. And you did already drive her like, nine hundred miles in the past couple of days. But I do appreciate you asking."

Calamity was now *vastly* overdue on an oil change and whined at me before roaring to life. It was honestly a miracle she had survived another road trip. I backed out of the driveway and turned right, exiting our subdivision and heading down the highway I knew by heart. With any luck they'd still have my visitor paperwork on file, even though I hadn't been to visit since I graduated high school.

The big gray building with high metal fences was about seven miles past city limits, with a sign declaring it was a *correctional center*, as if that would soften the reality that it was a prison and most of the people inside would never be free again. Some of them deserved it. Some of them, though, were good people who made a bad life choice—fucked up once and suffered for it forever.

Nerves fluttered in my stomach as I parked and headed inside, even though I had walked this path so many times before. Prisoners only got seven visits per calendar month, but January was a clean slate, with only a single day in the books. Surely Dad hadn't been here yet. I slid my driver's license and social security card across the counter, rattling off my mother's inmate number, something I still had committed to memory. I rented a locker for a dollar, putting Hesper's keys and my wallet and phone inside, and let a guard pat me down after walking through a metal detector.

I held my paper pass up and another guard buzzed me in, and God, the visiting room was just as awful as I remembered, with a long, low table dividing inmates and their families, hard plastic chairs, and a line of vending machines. I swiped the white card through the reader and picked out a soda, a bag of chips, and a candy bar. Had anyone else bought her snacks while I'd been in Pennsylvania? It was the only non-prison food she could have.

She beamed when she saw me. Her hair was more silver than black now, cut shorter than I remembered, curling around her face. And despite the unfairness of it all, my equally split anger at her and the broken system, I had to admit prison had done the one thing she never had the willpower to do herself: sobriety.

She hugged me across the table, and I held tight, squeezing hard as tears gathered in my eyes.

"Hi, Mom," I whispered, pulling back. Physical contact was highly discouraged.

"Your father didn't tell me you were coming home!"

"It was, um. An impromptu trip."

She gave me the eagle eye—the one that could detect

bullshit a mile away—but let it slide. "I see."

Instead of bringing up the fact that I never wrote, she leaned across the table, staring raptly at my face, still the best listener. Still my biggest fan.

"He *did* tell me about your knee though," she said softly. "I'm sorry."

"In some ways, I am...and in some ways, I'm not." The words were surprisingly true. I leaned forward on my elbows, bracing myself for the words I'd come here to say. "It used to make me so angry when Dad would say that everything happens for a reason. That there are more moving parts than we can ever see, and we can't possibly know how they all work together to move the future. And yeah, what happened to my knee was awful. It was the worst physical pain I've ever lived through, but it was more than that. I lost my scholarship, my dorm, my future. I didn't think I had anything. But y'know who was there to pick me back up?"

She smiled slyly. "I think I do, but go ahead and tell me anyway."

"Hesper."

When I said her name, Mom's eyes lit up, a grin showing off the dimples I'd inherited.

"She didn't let me quit. She...found a way."

"She's tougher than she seems."

"I've figured that out. And what started out as...as sort of a marriage of convenience—" Her eyebrows shot up, but I plowed on. "—made me realize maybe I had to lose some things to gain others. That the reason I was never happy with any other girl was it was never the girl I really wanted, and if losing my career and suffering the pain of healing meant I got to fall in love with my best friend, maybe that was a sacrifice I was okay with."

"You actually married Hesper Stalides."

"Yes."

"For...convenience."

I hung my head. "For free tuition, to be honest."

"But you *are* in love with her?"

"I, uh. I kind of suspect I always have been."

She laughed. "You spent every waking minute together, and when she moved across the country, you went *with* her."

"Yeah, everyone saw it coming but me."

"I just have one question." She leaned across the table, her smile fading, her expression earnest. "Are you happy, Felix?"

It was a loaded question. It was easy to say yes when I thought of the quiet domesticity, making jokes and eating Thai food and standing outside in the snow. But there was the quiet despair that settled over her sometimes, and all I could do was ride it out beside her. There was the terror when I realized she was *gone* the night of the gala, the realization I could lose her forever. The fact that I would never get to kiss her, that I would have to do a balancing act for the rest of my life to make sure I wasn't pushing her boundaries.

At the end of the day, when I weighed the good things against the hard things, when I asked myself if it was worth it...the answer was yes. Always yes.

"It's scary. And hard. There are things I have to give up to be with her. But...I'm happy. *We're* happy."

"Good. That's all that matters to me. But can you make me a promise?"

"Of course."

She hesitated. "I'm under two thousand now."

I didn't have to ask what she meant. The maximum sentence was fifteen years. She had less than five years left to go—five years until her sentence was up and she could come home to Dad, to whatever kids remained. By then, Molly, Anita, and Logan would probably already be gone. She'd left seven kids behind and would come home to three recalcitrant teenagers who didn't even remember her.

"If you and Hesper are still together, still happy—will you hold a ceremony? I've missed so much, I know, but...I want a chance to be there."

I found a spot on the wall behind her to stare at, measuring my breaths, because the familiar, ugly flash of anger washed through my veins.

If you didn't want to miss your kids growing up and getting married, maybe you shouldn't have gotten plastered and tried to drive home.

It wasn't fair—none of it was.

But she was a different person now; we all were. I had to let it go.

"Yeah," I agreed softly. "We'll have a ceremony. How many days, Mom?"

It was the first time I'd actually asked.

"One thousand, seven hundred and thirty-three."

"I think that's plenty of time to plan a wedding."

She gave me a watery smile, her complexion clear and glowing, no longer tinged by the constant flush of alcohol. "Thank you, Felix. It means a lot."

I swallowed, finally relinquishing the words I'd withheld in anger for so many years. "I love you, Mom."

Even at my lowest, when I denied it with every breath,

when I thought of the accident and the girl whose family had to bury her so young, when I thought of having to half-raise Logan and my sisters—even then, it had always been true. The years had changed her. They had changed me too. All we could do was keep moving forward.

And someday, she'd be there again. Free.

THE NEXT DAY, Jasmine booked a flight back to Pennsylvania and Hesper and I made the hour's drive with her to Lambert Airport. She sat in the middle, her duffel bag balanced on her lap, her fingers tapping lightning-fast on her phone.

"Are you sure you'll be okay?"

"I'm right here." I peered over at her. "You know that, right? I'm not going to let anything bad happen."

"I didn't ask you, I asked *her*."

Hesper smiled, pulling into the drop-off lane. "Yes, Jasmine, I'm sure."

"Because I can stay."

"I have eight Morlans watching my back. You get back to Tamry."

She grinned sheepishly, ducking her head. "Is it that obvious?"

Jasmine held an arm out—and Hesper, to my surprise, gingerly leaned in for the offered hug. Her voice was barely above a whisper.

"I'll keep everyone at Morrow off your back, and if you need me, just call."

"Gotcha. Thank you."

"And I'm really proud of you for standing up to that asshole."

Hesper let out a noise that was half-laugh, half-sob. "Don't count your chickens before they hatch. The hearing hasn't happened yet."

"I believe in you. You'll testify, and you'll do just fine."

I opened my door and hopped out of Calamity, letting Jasmine scoot out behind me. She unexpectedly threw an arm around me too.

"Take care of each other. I haven't forgotten the dubious origins of your marriage, but I'm pretty sure it's for real now, and this hearing will be a nightmare."

I swallowed. "I know."

She headed for the sliding glass doors and blew a kiss over her shoulder before disappearing inside. Hesper beeped the horn impatiently and I climbed back in, folded her fingers carefully in mine, and let the cold January sunshine wash over us. Somewhere in the back of my mind, a clock was ticking down the days and hours and minutes until the hearing, but for now, everything was okay.

"I don't think I've said it yet." She flipped on her blinker, craning her neck to see out into traffic as she merged back into the flow.

"Said what?"

"That I love you," she said casually, as if this was no big deal. As if it were obvious.

It was a good thing I wasn't driving. It was like a galaxy exploded in my brain.

"Close your mouth." Despite her sass, she smiled. "This isn't news."

"It's news to *me*."

"Anyway. I just thought I should tell you." She lifted her shoulders in a shrug. We took the exit back toward Tegan Creek. "Let's get back. No telling what kind of trouble Jackson and Molly are into."

Not even that could distract me from the revelation.

Hesper loved me.

And I loved her too.

CHAPTER FIFTEEN

HESPER

WE DIDN'T HAVE to be in court until 2:00 p.m., but we'd been there all afternoon. The four of us sat in line, huddled in hard plastic chairs outside the courtroom—Felix on my left, his arm protectively slung across the back of my chair, and Molly on my right, holding my hand on one side and Jackson's on the other. Across the room, a woman in a narrow skirt with glasses and a blonde chignon drummed her fingers against the paperwork in her hand, watching the door for any sign of Ray. She was a *victim's advocate*. I was hung between hating that—being labeled as a *victim*—and being so grateful I could weep. Officer Jeffries perched on a chair beside her, his mouth set in a grim line.

"What do you call a short trial in court?" Felix's voice was a low murmur, and I smiled in spite of myself, elbowing him. "A brief case."

"Not your best."

"Yeah, I'm kind of short on court puns. Luckily, I've never needed them." His smile faded. "Really though. How are you doing?"

I swallowed, focusing on the elaborate pattern in the tile on the floor instead of the muscles pulled so taut in my neck and shoulders I could hardly move. "I mean, I've spent my whole adult life trying to avoid exactly this situation. I could be better."

"I won't tell you it will be fine. It might not be fine, and it'll definitely be scary. But what I can tell you is that I'm here, okay?"

"I know."

My mouth was dry, my face was hot despite the January chill. Every ugly thing Ray had ever said to me looped on repeat in my ears.

You're stupid
You're lazy
You're worthless
You're useless
You're ugly
Failure
Ungrateful
Loser
Pathetic
Bitch

I put my head in my hands, trying to steady my breathing. This wasn't even the hard part. I hadn't testified yet. I hadn't had to face him.

"You can do this."

I didn't *want* to. But it was the only way to stop living in fear. It was the only way to move forward.

"Stalides?" A clerk called us in, marking the previous case as complete in the docket.

Unlike the judge in Pennsylvania, everyone here knew *exactly* how to pronounce my last name—because everyone knew Ray. Every cop, every judge and court security officer. I sat down and tucked my feet under the bench. Molly and Felix held my hands so tightly they started to go numb, anchoring me when Ray walked through the door. Wearing his uniform despite his suspension, his badge gleaming on his chest and his gun belt at his hip. Empty though—there was some satisfaction in that. The emergency order ensured he couldn't carry a weapon. He removed his hat in a mockery of respect and took a seat on the far side of the room.

"Petitioner, please come forward."

My hands shook. I wasn't sure my legs would hold me. Felix squeezed my hand, running his thumb across the gold band on my ring finger, a reminder. *For better or worse.* I took one step, then another, until I was standing before the judge, a balding older man with a nasal voice but a kind smile.

"Please state your name for the record."

"Hesper Stalides."

"Be seated."

I collapsed into the wooden chair on the platform beside the judge's bench. He silently read over my petition, carefully written out with the victim's advocate's help. His brow furrowed.

"Respondent, please come forward."

Ray sauntered up to the front. He stated his name per the judge's request, but his gaze never left me. His mouth was drawn down, and there were circles under his eyes. He was the picture of a remorseful, grieving, *wronged* man.

"An emergency order was issued on January 1st. The following day, a petition for a plenary order was filed." He shuffled his papers and cleared his throat.

He was going to read it out loud.

My breathing was too fast and ragged, my lungs squeezing, desperate for air. My skin burned; I was on fire from the inside out—

I locked eyes with Felix, focused on the familiar crease between his eyebrows, on all the lines of his face, which I knew better than my own. I timed my breaths with his as the judge read my words back, every hellish detail included.

"Petitioner, please rise and repeat after me. I swear the evidence and testimony that I shall give shall be the truth, the whole truth and nothing but the truth, so help me God."

My voice was clearer than I expected, stronger and louder, when I parroted the oath back.

"Do you have any testimony or evidence to add to this case?"

"I would like to submit these photos." I slid a manila envelope across the bench with trembling hands. "They confirm my story. You can see the bruises on my arms where he grabbed me, the black eyes where I hit the cage of the squad car he used to abduct me." I hesitated.

All or nothing. This was my only chance to make my

case, to be heard. To stop hiding and let the world know what I had been through. What I had survived.

"But this is only the latest in a lifelong string of abuse."

There was not a sound in the courtroom. I closed my eyes against the prickle of tears, hot shame and embarrassment and a strange and vicious vindication that my voice was finally, finally being heard.

"I grew up being told I was nothing, and I believed it. He would tell me I was being stupid, selfish, terrible—then tell me it was my fault I was upset, because I was just too sensitive." The tears were tracking down my cheeks now. I looked out at the empty seats; Jo had, ultimately, not come to help fight this battle. But that was okay. I had enough fight in me for both of us. "And I didn't tell people, because why would they believe me? All he had to do was say I was just a bratty kid, and everyone would roll their eyes. I thought it really *was* my fault."

"She is *lying under oath—*" Ray thundered, but he was interrupted.

"You will have the opportunity for testimony after the petitioner is finished," the judge cautioned.

"I thought things could be different; that I could have a better life, that I could be free. I moved across the country. I didn't tell people where I went. I was so careful. But it wasn't enough."

My stomach clenched and I wrapped my arms around myself, trying not to heave. "He had one of his friends stalk me all the way across the country. He sent me unwanted letters in the mail. He called and harassed me, tried to make me feel guilty and small and stupid like he always did. He had someone break into my house. He bought his way into a college event he knew I would be attending." I held up another envelope, this one containing a DVD Jasmine had mailed to me. "And he hauled me away—I have the security footage—with the intent of keeping me under his control for the rest of my life. He wanted me to be afraid. He wanted me under his thumb. He wanted to gaslight me into believing every horrible thing he's ever said about me, then turn around and make me feel responsible."

Ray's eyes blazed, his jaw clenched. It was more than the arrogance and condescension I was used to; this was an inferno, reined in only because he was still trying to save face.

The DVD was damning evidence. So were the photographs of the fresh bruises, which had finally faded to a pale, sickly yellow-brown shade on my arms. There was nothing he could do to argue against it. It made me, for the first time, *brave*.

"He has terrorized me every moment of my life. He used his police vehicle to pull me over in high school; he used his authority to pull strings in any way he could to keep me under his thumb. And when he thought I got away? He came after me. And all I want, all I've ever wanted, is for him to leave me alone. For this abuse to stop. For people to understand that law enforcement might be his job, but that does not make him a good man—and he shouldn't get a free pass because of it."

The judge accepted the photos into evidence, his brow creasing. Somewhere, far off in the distance, Jeffries confirmed their validity, but all I heard was the rush of blood in my ears, the furious beating of my heart, the screaming gale of fear and triumph because *I was finally saying these things out loud*, and someone might finally believe me.

Ray stood for his testimony, and I braced my arms against the chair, my stomach curdling at the sound of his voice, oily and sweet once again.

"Your Honor, my daughter needs *help*, help that I was just trying to give her."

"I need clarification. Help for what, exactly?" The judge peered over to him.

"She ran away from home—"

"She left home as a legal adult, correct?"

Ray *hated* to be interrupted. His sharp intake of breath betrayed his temper. "She was eighteen, yes, but she was not, *is not*, capable of living alone. I just want her to have a safe, structured environment. I brought her home to protect her. You can see that she needs some stability; this whole ordeal is nothing more than the temper tantrum of a child. I have every right to do what's best for my daughter!"

My cheeks burned, because this was how it started. He planted a seed of doubt and insisted his intentions were good. He discredited me so they wouldn't believe me.

He would win. He would walk away. *I knew it.*

"And the physical evidence?" the judge asked; the skepticism in his voice gave me hope.

Ray's eyes gleamed. "I didn't leave those bruises. They were there when I picked her up."

Officer Jeffries stood up. "If you play the DVD, Your Honor, you'll see the security footage where he dragged her to his vehicle. There were no bruises on her arms or face at that time. It also clearly shows she was taken against her will; she was combative."

"Anyone could have doctored a video," Ray scoffed, but

Jeffries talked right over him.

"I contacted Morrow College and received a copy directly from their security office. I can confirm the chain of custody. I was on-scene when Ms. Stalides left the property; she was terrified, and with good reason."

Finally.

"This hearing will have to be continued at a later date," Ray demanded. "I wasn't prepared to deal with these outrageous claims!"

"The respondent does not schedule court dates," the judge thundered. "There will be no continuation. Do you have any more testimony to give? Any evidence to support your claims?"

Everyone but Ray shrank back in their seats. "My word is support enough; I am *under oath*, I am an officer of the *law—*" he bellowed.

"I will grant the maximum allowable two-year plenary order of protection." He banged his gavel. "Criminal charges for unlawful restraint and battery will be issued by the State's Attorney. Mr. Stalides, you are hereby remanded into police custody for questioning." He stood from the bench.

Bailiffs who had been standing by the door moved forward cautiously. Neither of them would meet Ray's eyes. Did they know him? Had they worked with him before? They didn't attempt to handcuff him. He walked between them, his gait slow and even, his face bunched up as though he were about to cry, though there were no tears in his eyes.

"We'll clear up this misunderstanding and it will all be water under the bridge. I love you, Hesper."

My stomach churned, but I didn't lower my head. I had nothing to be ashamed of. "No," I whispered. "You don't."

Everything was muffled: the sights, the sounds. It was like trying to walk through water. I ambled by Felix numbly, felt his breath ruffle my hair as he followed on my heels when I walked out into the vestibule, then down the stairs, through the metal detector, and out into the afternoon sunshine, surprisingly warm despite the snow that had fallen over the last week. My legs wobbled and if a pair of gentle hands hadn't caught me by the elbows, I might have gone down right on the courthouse's front steps. Felix gingerly eased me down and sat beside me. He tossed Calamity's keys to Jackson and Molly, ushering them along.

It's over, it's over, it's over.

But it wasn't.

Molly came back from the Jeep and pressed something into my hands—my go-bag. For once I felt empty, like I had nothing to pour out onto the page. I flipped my sketchbook open and ran my fingers across the pages like a timeline. I found the trees I drew while Felix was in the hospital. I found a dozen iterations of his face, laughing and scowling with concentration and a few asleep, his lashes against his cheeks and his hair sticking up. Taped to the cardboard back cover was a strip of photo booth pictures we'd taken at the mall years ago, Felix and I making ridiculous faces at each other, and God, how could he not have known I was in love with him even then?

"It's not over." My voice was hoarse, though I hadn't been screaming—at least, I thought I hadn't.

"No," Felix agreed. "It isn't. But it's the beginning of the end. And we'll do it together."

For the first time, it felt *possible*. It felt like there was an end to the nightmare. I flopped backward on the concrete, an unexpected laugh bubbling out of me, and he laid back, too, his hand hovering over mine as if asking permission.

"We don't have to appear for the criminal trial here. We can just...go home," I whispered.

A small pang of sorrow squeezed at my lungs when I thought of leaving the rest of the Morlan family again, but it eased when I thought of my painting room, our bed, the little flower garden beside the house, the library at Morrow, of everything holding its breath, just waiting for us to come back.

I sat up again, sucking in the sharp, chilly air, smiling over at Felix.

"Let's see if Calamity can survive one more road trip to Pennsylvania."

EPILOGUE

FELIX

"I GUESS TUITION waivers don't extend to sisters-in-law, huh?"

Molly perched on the arm of the couch, one arm draped around Jackson's shoulders, her mouth pulled down in a frown. It was a Morlan Family Meeting, all of us crowded into the living room, Dad in his recliner presiding over us before we headed back home.

"No." Hesper was leaned back into my shoulder, too comfortable to sit up. "But there are scholarships and campus jobs."

"And if you're going to run off to college, at least it'll be somewhere your brother can keep an eye on you," Dad added ruefully, and he gave Jackson a look that could peel paint. "And Mr. Maddox here doesn't go there, so he won't distract you from your classes."

Pearcy was only an hour's drive. I was sure they'd make time to see each other. Molly had been waitressing in Tegan Creek and working weekend shifts at the music store the next town over, saving up for college, and now she had decided she wanted to join us on the east coast in a few months and go to Morrow in the fall.

Anita and Logan exchanged a *look*.

"I'll be back," Molly promised, but we all knew it wasn't true. She'd been living with one foot out the door for years, ready for her next big adventure, to seize whatever life had in store for her next.

"You can fly back for Thanksgiving and Christmas," Jackson offered.

He was met with uncomfortable silence. Flights were expensive; *holiday* flights were even worse.

"We'll figure something out." Molly shrugged.

Hesper stood up, stretching her arms over her head. "I hate to ruin the party, but we've got a long drive ahead of us."

We'd drop Jackson at the airport like we'd done for Jasmine a couple of weeks ago—"with all due respect, dude, I can fly in two hours, I'm not riding in that hunk of junk for eight hours again," he'd said—and then we'd have the trip to ourselves. When Jackson stood up, Molly fisted her hands in the front of his shirt and yanked him down to her eye level, his eyes widening in surprise.

"When I get to Morrow, you owe me a date," she said

sternly.

Anita tugged on the back of her shirt, urging her to sit back down, but she wasn't deterred, yanking him down a little further and kissing him. He flailed helplessly for a moment, acutely aware of Dad's and Logan's murderous glares and Janie's, Jetta's, and Jules's gleeful shrieks, before she let him go, patting his cheek fondly and grinning.

"Double dates with Felix and Hesper *only*," Dad shouted, but Molly just rolled her eyes.

They piled around for a group hug, then we trooped out of the door.

"*Don't* call Calamity a hunk of junk," Hesper snapped, glaring at Jackson, who was still a bit dazed.

"If the shoe fits..." He let me in the passenger door first, then hopped in beside me.

As we drove out of city limits, Hesper's hands tightened on the steering wheel. Ray's police car still sat in his driveway. The lights were on in the house; he was home. He hadn't even spent the night in jail. He had probably laughed it off with his pals, *you know how kids are, she's so dramatic*, and they'd probably gone out for a beer. My lungs ached. It was hard to breathe past the realization that the world wasn't fair and some things would never change.

But *Hesper* had changed.

Though she tensed, her face was determined, unafraid. She smiled over at me.

Things were gonna be okay.

To keep Jackson quiet, she rolled down the windows and let me pick a CD out of the binder she kept under the seat. I found a burned one covered with my handwriting, one I'd made her ages ago, and popped it into the stereo. The swell of guitars and the thumping bass filled Calamity, and to my surprise, Jackson joined us in singing along, practically shouting to be heard over the wind.

Unlike Jasmine, he didn't give us hugs or wish us luck at the airport. He just got out, waved briefly, and started jogging for the doors.

"Guess we better head that way." I stretched, enjoying the extra room Jackson had vacated. "Unless there's something you want to do in St. Louis before we go...?"

"The coupons you made me for Christmas—are they still valid if I can't present them at the time of purchase?"

I stared at her, confused, her face pale but shining with a tentative smile.

"One of them was for a museum date. Our gala date got interrupted, so I thought—"

"Yes," I blurted. "The coupon is valid."

Her hand drifted to the seat between us and I folded my fingers around hers, carefully, loosely so that she could pull away if she wanted. But she didn't. I rubbed my thumb in slow circles across the back of her hand, and she turned back into traffic, headed for Forest Park. Admission to the museum was free, and as broke teenagers we spent hours there on weekends, sitting on benches and soaking up the history and wonder.

This time was different. Hesper tugged me by the hand as she raced up the stone steps, dwarfed by the enormous pillars and statues on top of them. DEDICATED TO ART AND FREE TO ALL, the entryway proclaimed. We had done this before, but mostly while I played on my phone and she gazed adoringly at impressive artwork. We walked from room to room, hand in hand, and she explained things she'd already told me more than once, but that was okay. That was fine.

"They have the Monet out," she whispered reverently. "And two Van Goghs—"

"Hesper."

"—*The Stairway at Auvers!*"

"Hesper." This time she turned to look at me, her eyes bright, bruises masked behind makeup Molly had spent the morning applying. She drifted toward the paintings like they had a gravitational pull, but I held on to her hand, anchoring her in my orbit. My palms were sweaty. I didn't have a ring. This was not how this was supposed to go, but the words wouldn't stop. "I love you. I'm *in* love with you. And I want to marry you."

She held up her hand in confusion, her mother's wedding band shining in the display lights. "But—"

"For real this time. In sickness and in health. For better or for worse." I swallowed. "I mean it."

A few months ago, a few weeks ago, even, she might have paused. She might have listed off on her fingers all the things she thought would turn me away from her. She might have doubted that I meant it.

"Yes."

"Yes?"

"Yes, I will marry you."

I swept her up into my arms and she laughed, her smile radiant as she threaded her fingers through my hair, and oh, God, I'd tear the tendon in my knee a thousand times if that's what it took for her to look at me like that.

I'd get her a real ring. We'd have a ceremony and invite

her mother and the entire Morlan clan. We'd go on a honey-moon—no expectations, no pushing boundaries, just having adventures and making memories.

And we'd live happily ever after.

ACKNOWLEDGEMENTS

First and foremost, I have to thank Avalynne Lewis, my life-long partner in crime, best friend, and alpha reader. I don't know what I'd do without you, Avi; you make the world a better place and I'm so glad you're in it. I'd also like to thank Tara Garrett, Debbie Burrow, Catherine Bakewell, Erin Elizabeth Grammar, Kayla Martin-Gant, Bronwen Write and Kirsten Maier, who always believed in me more than I believed in myself. A special thank you to Anna Stein, My Person.

Extra shout-out to my beloved book-Twitter friends and beta readers; without you all this would never have existed. You share inspirational snippets, bring joy to my life, and make me feel like I deserve the space I take up in the world. Thank you, thank you, thank you.

About Lucy Mason

Lucy lives in rural southern Illinois with a frankly ridiculous amount of yarn and books. During the day she works in adult education and by night she's a writer and dabbler in yarncrafts. She knits, loves video games and podcasts, and cries over fictional characters regularly.

Email
lucymason217@gmail.com

Twitter
@LucyMason217

Website
www.lucymasonwrites.wordpress.com

CONNECT WITH NINESTAR PRESS

WWW.NINESTARPRESS.COM

WWW.FACEBOOK.COM/NINESTARPRESS

WWW.FACEBOOK.COM/GROUPS/NINESTARNICHE

WWW.TWITTER.COM/NINESTARPRESS

WWW.INSTAGRAM.COM/NINESTARPRESS

Made in the USA
Middletown, DE
07 August 2023

36330110R00146